PEWTER CREEK MOUNTAIN

K. D. Gearhart

Cover design by E.C. Stever

Cover Photo credit Victor Tongdee

Print ISBN: 978-1-098598-35-8

DEDICATION

Norma "Gail" (Hemler) O'Haver
September 23, 1921 – December 15, 2010

For my mother, who taught me
"Words Open the World to You"

ACKNOWLEDGMENTS

"The Good, The Bad, and The Ugly"

The title of the 1966 movie encapsulates my writing journey of *Pewter Creek Mountain*. Why—because I wrote good stuff, bad stuff, and UGLY stuff.

Thank you to the many who helped me make the dream of becoming a published author a reality: my husband, Tom; Bearlodge Writers from Sundance, Wyoming; Black Hills Fiction Writers from Spearfish, South Dakota; beta readers Kathy Kovar (check out K. L. Kovar on Amazon) and Carolyn Helget. Thank you to my editor Jennifer Goode Stevens for making my writing better. A VERY special thank you to Eric Stever (follow Eric at E.C. Stever on Amazon) who without his techy savvy, this manuscript would still be collecting dust on my desk.

And last but not least, I want to thank my mother who though she never realized her dream of becoming an author, works through me to create characters and plot lines I hope you enjoy.

PROLOGUE

Tuesday morning

THE RISING SUN crept over the horizon and shone through the windshield. Troy Edwards turned his head away from the penetrating light and slid out of the Jeep Wrangler onto the edge of the gravel road. As he stretched his cramped muscles, a meadowlark trilled to announce its presence from a nearby barbed-wire fence. Troy's blue-jean-clad knee brushed against a clump of sagebrush as he stepped aside to swing the door closed. The pungent odor reminded him of deer hunting in Wyoming with his granddad, and of the taste of his grandmother's venison dressing. The lark took flight as

Troy flipped open the back of the Jeep to pull out a bottle of water and a protein bar. He leaned against the black vehicle and scanned the panorama before him—miles of sun-bleached prairie swelled like ocean waves to crash into the purple triangles of a mountain range.

"A change of scenery might not be a bad idea," the counselor had stated, clipboard and pen gently laid on the table beside his chair to signal the hour was up. At the time, Troy scoffed at the suggestion, silently reassuring himself he could handle a few unsettling nightmares. He just needed to suck it up. But as the scene of blood, brain matter, and bone fragments became a nightly visitor, Troy had tossed camping gear into the Jeep and headed out. For the past three days he had driven roads less traveled—eaten when he was hungry, catnapped when he was tired—not bothering to set up camp. Last night he had driven down this deserted country road just as the moon made its appearance.

A conversation overheard at a gas pump just inside the Colorado border from Kansas had piqued his interest ". . . hiking trails on Pewter Creek Mountain are insane!" A Google search showed the town of Pewter Creek at the base of the mountain bearing the same name. Troy swiped through the Chamber of Commerce pictures—a snow-capped mountain; the sky ablaze with oranges and pinks at sunset; backpackers high-fiving at the top of a trail; a mountain biker silhouetted against a thick green forest; a smiling fly fisherman in hip waders holding up a twelve-inch rainbow trout; a family of four standing beside snowmobiles; and lastly a bird's-eye view of Pewter Creek snaking its pewter-colored path down the mountain to S-curve through the rustic town. The town's website boasted of heated arguments over which came first—the name of the town, the name of the creek, or the name of the mountain. At least one murder in the late 1800s had resulted from one such argument! About the controversy, Troy could not have cared less. He just wanted solitary camping and healing.

The empty water bottle and wrapper stowed in a sack on the passenger floorboard, Troy whistled a nameless tune as he opened his atlas and calculated the mileage to his destination. He was glad he'd picked up the map, as he was in the land of no cell service. Excitement built at the thought of pitching his tent wherever he wanted tonight. It had been too many years since he'd had any choices. *Over there,* all the decisions were made for you, right down to the time you were allotted to squat over a hastily dug latrine.

The Jeep dipped into a jarring hole as Troy backed around, sending the dog tags that hung from the rearview mirror swaying. He reached up and steadied the sun-warmed metal, thinking, *Trace, I really miss you, buddy.*

CHAPTER 1

THE SMELL OF URINE clung to Zane Butler. He palm-rubbed his eyes, blinked, and rubbed again. His tongue made a sucking noise against the roof of his mouth. The taste was foul. And dry—a 12-pack of beer dry.

Zane shivered. The August sunrise on Pewter Creek Mountain was chilly, and he was dressed only in cargo shorts and a Butler Sporting Goods T-shirt. Head pounding, he grabbed the bed of the all-terrain vehicle and pulled himself up from the ground where he had passed out, back leaning against the ATV's knobby tire. His shorts were stiff where urine had chilled and dried.

The chatter of a squirrel startled him, and he whirled in the direction of the sound. "Little bastard," he shouted.

His breath hung in the air like a snort from an angry bull, and he clambered into the Polaris RZR and turned the key. Relieved when the motor purred, he leaned his forehead against the steering wheel, eyes closed against the brightness of the day. Snippets of last night's events flickered like a movie trailer across his eyelids. He flipped open the cooler on the passenger seat and pawed through it looking for a beer, cursing a blue streak when his search came up empty. He jammed the gearshift into drive. The engine lugged, and the 1,200-pound machine stayed put. Putting it in reverse stalled the engine.

"Son of a bitch."

Zane slid off the black vinyl seat and dropped to his knees to peer at the undercarriage.

What he saw sent him scrambling backward, a trail of vomit in his wake. He clawed at his shorts pocket and retrieved his cell phone. The call was answered on the first ring, and Zane squeaked out, "I need help."

CHAPTER 2

JESSIE BUTLER'S FORD F-150 growled as it steadily climbed Pewter Creek Mountain. She wished now she'd taken time to make coffee before leaving the house, but Zane's call had left her worried—*I need help*. It had taken several minutes of Zane's incoherent babbling before she understood he was on Pewter Mountain, down U.S. Forest Service Road 222.

Jessie made good time on the graveled County Road 37. She pulled into Iron Trailhead, a large parking area that signaled the end of the county's responsibility and the beginning of the Forest Service's domain. From there, a trail system that resembled octopus tentacles reached out into the heavily wooded, rugged terrain. A frown crossed her face at the graffiti defacing the Plexiglass that covered the trail map.

Jessie buzzed the window down as she crept past the familiar brown-and-white Forest Service sign that said FS 222 would intersect with FS 186 in five miles. What the sign didn't say was that FS 222 was a series of switchbacks that snaked up to the summit of Pewter Creek Mountain before falling quickly down the other side to FS 186.

Jessie slowed to a crawl as she turned onto the rutted, narrow road used primarily by ATVs in the summer, snowmobilers in the winter, and mountain bikers all year round. She wondered what trouble Zane had gotten into this time. And, more importantly, how much it would cost her. She had been hopeful that, with his recent marriage to Mary Beth, her 30-year-old son would finally stop with his high-school shenanigans.

Zane rushed his mother's pickup, jerking the door open before she came to a complete stop behind his ATV angled off the trail. She wrinkled her nose at the smell of stale beer and urine.

"What I've done—it's bad this time, Mom."

"You think it's bad every time," she said, her tone soft and reassuring. Flies buzzed away as Jessie stepped over the vomit toward the front of the machine. "Get high-centered on a fallen rock?" she asked, tapping a large boulder that had tumbled off the rock wall along the road. Then she saw the mangled mountain bike.

"Not a rock," Zane said, his voice scarcely above a whisper. "A body."

CHAPTER 3

ELDON JOHNSON'S MORNING had started early, just after sunrise. The number on his caller ID had made his heart jump and sent a twitch to his morning wood. Instead of the hoped-for booty call, however, he heard, "I'm down FS 222. And Eldon, bring a shovel."

He'd driven up to see Jessie standing alone, away from the blue and white all-terrain vehicle. Tapping the bed of the Polaris, he asked, "Isn't this Zane's? What's it stuck on?" He bent to look under the machine. He immediately staggered back, the two breakfast burritos he had scarfed down on the way up the mountain joining Zane's splatter from earlier.

"Jesus Christ, Eldon. Get a grip."

Eldon gave Jessie a hard look and strode to his pickup, where he retrieved his coffee cup, leaving the door ajar. He took a big mouthful, swished and spit in the dirt. He walked back to where Jessie stood. "Now, what the hell happened up here?"

Jessie ignored his question. "Pull the pickup past the front of the machine," she said.

He asked a second time. "What happened?"

Ignoring him again, Jessie brushed past Eldon toward his pickup, her cowboy boots leaving deep imprints in the powdery black dirt. He called after her, "Did Zane do this? Was he drunk again?"

She whirled around and gave him a narrow-eyed glare, but then her shoulders rounded in defeat. "I don't know exactly what happened. Zane called me. I came up here, found him a mess, and sent him home in my pickup. And then I called you to come help me because . . ." Jessie's voice trailed off. She sat heavily on Eldon's running board and gestured for the coffee cup he still held.

He handed it to her. "Did you call Harold? I think the meat wagon's in the shop, but he could probably borrow the hearse."

"No."

"No, what? You didn't call Harold, or he can't borrow the hearse?"

"We aren't calling anyone. None of us—Zane, me, you—can afford this kind of attention right now with the election just four months away." Shaking her head, she added, "Too much to lose."

Eldon reached past Jessie to pull a bottle of Jim Beam from under the seat. After a long pull, he handed the bottle to her and she followed suit. Eldon removed his cowboy hat and mopped his sweaty forehead with his shirt sleeve. "Jessie, have you thought this through?"

Silence.

Eldon squished a black beetle as it approached the toe of his Tony Lama. "Easy to explain it away. Always getting tree huggers up here hiking and crazy mountain bikers riding in the dark with a weak headlamp. Sharp curve in the road. Pow!" Eldon smacked his fist into the palm of his hand. "Unavoidable accident."

Jessie stood and motioned for Eldon to follow her back to the ATV. She picked up a forked tree branch and waited for him to join her. The front tire rested against the torso of a young woman, her lower half hidden underneath the machine. Jessie moved the stick over the body like a divining rod, stopping at the ragged hole in her chest.

"How do you explain away a bullet hole?"

CHAPTER 4

HIGH, THIN CLOUDS were playing peek-a-boo with the sun by the time Jessie and Eldon drove off the mountain. The forecast promised rain by the afternoon, with periods of heavier precipitation throughout the night.

"Get cleaned up and go to work. Business as usual," had been Jessie's parting words to Eldon before she roared away on the ATV, leaving a dust trail floating in the heavy air.

"'Bout time the second-highest-paid sheriff's department employee showed up for work. Good morning, Eldon. And you look like shit."

"Give it a rest, Geraldine," Deputy Eldon Johnson

growled as he passed the receptionist's desk and entered the sanctuary of the office he shared with his boss.

He came right back out.

"Jesus Christ!" he roared, holding up a plastic sack.

"Well if you hadn't been in such a huff, I would have told you Crazy Clara brought you in a present this morning," Geraldine said. "She said someone was out by her cabin during the night shooting everything that moved. One of her pet squirrels was a casualty, and she brought you pieces and parts to prove it. Do you want me to send the victim to the lab for DNA results?"

Geraldine reached for the bag, obviously enjoying herself—something she did every chance she got at his expense. She had known Eldon since he was a baby and had even changed his diapers, and she never missed the chance to share that information in mixed company.

"Don't call me, I'll call you," he growled over his shoulder as he pushed through the glass door, leaving Geraldine's laughter behind.

His gut burned from the whiskey, and his arm muscles screamed from the simple movement of climbing into the pickup. *Screw work,* he thought as he drove toward downtown Pewter Creek and away from the brick building that housed the sheriff's department.

It was just past ten—Rosie's Diner would still be serving breakfast. Eldon parked in the diner's half-full parking lot. He grimaced as he pushed the pickup door shut with his elbow, just as Vince Humphreys stepped off the sidewalk into the parking lot. "Morning, Deputy."

"Vince. You working today?"

"Yup. Jason's on early shift. I'm working the eleven-to-six." Vince motioned across the street to the empty parking spaces in front of Butler's Sporting Goods Store. "I think Jason can handle the customers. Buy you a cup of coffee, a cinnamon roll? Looks like we'll be just in time for the morning BS session. Wonder who's the topic of conversation today? Probably something to do with the upcoming election. Your boss getting worried?"

"Naw." Eldon halted in mid-stride. "On second thought, thinking about those old farts gossiping has made me lose my appetite. Rain check?"

"Sure thing." Vince stared at the middle-aged, overweight deputy as he climbed back into the county pickup, gunned the engine, and bounced over the curb—not bothering to use the parking lot exit. *Odd—not like Eldon to pass up a free cup of coffee. Or a cinnamon roll.*

Vince decided to pass on the gossip, too, and walked down to the post office. He pulled two pieces of mail from his P.O. box—a renewal notice for *The Cobalt County News* and a handwritten, no-return-address envelope containing a letter addressed to "Dear Cobalt County Voter." It was from the sheriff wannabe, Wayne Sinclair. A smile widened across Vince's suntanned face. The upcoming sheriff's race just might add a little spice to this otherwise dull town.

Vince continued down the street to the parking lot

behind Butler's. He tossed the mail into his mud-encrusted Chevy pickup, which looked a little well-used parked next to Jason Mobley's immaculate gold Impala. The two men were as different as night and day, but they worked surprisingly well together as clerks in the store.

Vince scrunched up his face against the music that blared from the store's outdoor speakers. He knew the older customers didn't care for the noise—they'd sure told him often enough. Usually while they were asking why the manager (taking up TWO parking spaces) parks his diesel-puking, jacked-up, one-ton pickup with black-tinted windows and offensive bumper stickers (nothing funny about a boy peeing on a Chevy emblem or mud flaps depicting naked ladies) right in front of the store—instead of in the rear lot with the rest of the employees. "My peeps need to know Zane's in the house!" had been said manager's reply when Vince mentioned it.

Two years! The time left before Vince's Social Security kicked in. Then he could tell the Butler family to kiss his ass goodbye.

Zane wasn't "in the house" this morning, though. *Mr. Important too hung over to show up for work, or maybe the governor flew him down to the capital for some advice.* The thought made Vince chuckle aloud.

"Morning, Jason," Vince said after walking through the open store door and past the twenty-five-year-old slumped on a stool behind the cash register. Jason's bloodshot eyes and puffy face hovered over a Styrofoam container of half-eaten biscuits and gravy.

Jason sucked gravy from his mustache. "*Jutro*," he answered. "Croatian today," referring to a Facebook word-a-day challenge. Vince rolled his eyes and continued to the closet-sized office where the time clock hung on the wall. Crushed beer cans littered the area around the trash can; obviously there'd been no NBA stars among last night's drinkers.

"Smells like a brewery in there," Vince said returning to the register area. "And just so you know, I'm not cleaning the mess up."

"Only fair. I'll do it later. Drew stopped by yesterday afternoon. Guess we got a little wasted. He brought in some home brew, and then we got into Zane's favorite beer—Black Tooth Bomber Mountain."

"Boss too hung over to show up for work?"

Jason shrugged, closing the lid on the coagulated gravy mixture. "He called me early and asked me to open up. Said he had something to take care of today. Might leave you to close tonight too. Guess I'd better get the office cleaned up in case Mama Butler stops in."

CHAPTER 5

WELCOME TO PEWTER CREEK.

Marigolds bloomed beneath the town sign, flanked by short-clipped greenery starting to show a hint of fall. Troy idled the Jeep past the town welcome sign and down the main street into town, alternating looking right and left. He noticed a Forest Service ranger station on his right and debated stopping to pick up a camping permit and trails map. Deciding to check out the rest of the town first, a green-and-white sign told Troy he was crossing Pewter Creek. The downtown district began, on the right, with a brick building housing the United States Post

17

Office. It was situated next to the bank, whose sign wished Madison Williams a happy fifth birthday and then flashed the date and time—it was just shy of four-thirty. Across the street, a boarded-up storefront took up the space between Pearl's Curls and Randolph's Mortuary. A dog crossed in front of Troy to make use of the green space next to Rosie's Diner, which was sprinkled with picnic tables. Butler's Sporting Goods Store was on the corner across from the diner. Then the road split, with a sign pointing right to the recreational national forest. A left turn at the intersection led Troy around to the backside of the block; there was a bar on each corner, with *The Cobalt County News* and Hayward's Pharmacy in between. Troy circled around the business district, parked, and went into the ranger station. He smiled and thanked the friendly ranger, smartly dressed in olive green, as he stowed his new fourteen-day camping permit in his wallet. As he exited the building and stepped off the curb, a loud pop drove him into a crouch against the oversized front tire of his Jeep, his hand instinctively clutching at his right hip. Loud music blared from a passing pickup as another backfire cracked the air.

Troy stood, rubbed the sweat off his upper lip with his T-shirt sleeve and looked around, embarrassed at his response to the noise. He got in the Jeep and sat a few minutes with the door open, calming his breathing and letting his heart return to its normal rhythm before he started the engine and eased onto the road toward the grocery store. He turned into the lot, mentally making a grocery list.

Whoop. Whoop.

Troy glanced in his rearview mirror at the flashing lights in the grill of a Dodge pickup. The sun reflected off the Pewter Creek law enforcement emblem as the officer swung the door open and walked up to the driver's side window.

"You failed to signal your turn. License, registration, proof of insurance." Troy complied and then placed his hands on the steering wheel in plain sight. A few minutes later, the officer stood, feet splayed apart, at the window. "We might have a problem here, Mr. Troy Edwards. License plates come back to a Trace Richards. And his name, not yours, is on the registration."

"It was my buddy's Jeep, officer. Haven't had time to get the paperwork changed over. Okay if I reach into the glove compartment for the bill of sale?"

A curt nod was followed by, "You just passing through?"

"No, officer. Heading up Pewter Creek Mountain for some camping. Probably a little fishing and hiking too."

"Word of friendly advice, there's a weather front moving in. And our mountain is no place for a tourist." The last word was drawn out to three syllables. "It's easy to get turned around, and there are lots of rockslide areas that can cover up a body so deep even the scavengers can't find it."

Troy retrieved his paperwork, noting the name tag pinned above the shirt pocket. "Thank you for the advice." Troy called after the retreating uniform, "Ma'am, have a nice day."

Sheriff Jessie Butler was surprised that the door to the department office was unlocked. She glanced at the clock on the wall; it was close to five-thirty. The sheriff grimaced to see the reception desk occupied by Geraldine Penwell, just as it had been for the past thirty-one years. She had outlived three sheriffs and showed no signs of retirement.

"Geraldine, you should be home fixing Ernest his supper."

Geraldine rushed around her desk just as a middle-aged woman came out of the restroom, clutching a picture frame to her chest. "Sheriff, this is Madeline Granger. Her daughter, Chloe, is missing."

"Mrs. Granger," Jessie addressed the obviously upset woman. "You and your daughter live on the old Smith place north of town?"

Madeline looked to Geraldine as if she held the answer to the question. Geraldine nodded toward the sheriff. Madeline found her voice and answered, "Yes."

"Let's go into my office, and you can tell me your story." To Geraldine, she said, "You'd better go home to Ernest before he reports *you* missing." The joke fell flat.

With a frosty look at her boss, Geraldine retrieved her black purse from the bottom desk drawer and patted Madeline's arm as she passed. "Don't worry. Everything will be okay."

The sheriff followed Geraldine to the door and turned the deadbolt after her. After seating Madeline in the chair across from her desk, Jessie asked, "May I get you something to drink? Water?"

"No, thank you. I'm just so worried about Chloe." Madeline pulled a tissue from her cardigan pocket and swiped at her nose. "She left the house yesterday afternoon for a bike ride. She hasn't been home since. And she hasn't called." Madeline looked down at the picture in her lap before clutching it to her chest, reluctant to hand it over. "I don't have a recent picture of her. This is her college graduation photo. I kept telling her I needed a new one, but she doesn't like her picture taken. She's such—"

The sheriff interrupted. "Madeline, let's start with some information first." Jessie pulled a yellow tablet from the desk drawer and took a "Re-elect Sheriff Butler" pen from a cup on the corner of the desk. "Why did you move here last September?"

Startled at the question, Madeline asked, "What?"

"Just getting background on why a single woman would move to the mountains of Colorado just before winter. And buy an old isolated house in the country. This is a small community, and you've kept to yourself. It just seems odd you wouldn't join some clubs. A church. Something."

"What does that have to do with my missing Chloe?"

Jessie threw down the pen, exhaling loudly. "We won't get very far in finding your daughter if you answer every one of my questions with a question."

Madeline becoming more flustered, stammered, "I mean, on television shows they ask for age, physical description, and what she was wearing. Purple. Chloe always wears purple."

"And on TV they find the missing person within an hour between commercial breaks. That isn't real life. Nor is it how we do things in *my* town."

The sheriff leaned forward and picked up the pen. "Are you ready to give me some background on you and your daughter so I can begin to do my job?"

Madeline twisted the tissue between her fingers. "Kent, my husband . . ." She stopped, and her deep inhale whistled in the quietness of the room. "Kent passed away after a three-year battle with cancer. We, Chloe and I, took care of him at home until the end. We don't have any other family, just each other. Chloe's an only child. She unselfishly divided her time between earning a college degree, and later a job, and helping me take care of her father.

"After Kent was gone, I couldn't make myself stay in the house. Everything was a painful reminder of him. I tried moving to an apartment, but everywhere I went something would trigger a memory. The ghost of Kent drove down every street with me, shared the booth at restaurants with me. Even seeing his favorite box of cereal in the grocery store brought on anxiety attacks. I was a mess, but Chloe was there with me every second, sacrificing her own life.

"One day I was going through the photo album, and I ran across the pictures of a trip Kent and I had taken. He had snapped a picture of a flower we saw on Pewter Creek Mountain." With pride in her voice, she said, "He was quite an accomplished photographer. Looking at that picture—it was like I could smell the sweet richness of the fragrance all over again. Something changed in me. I wanted to move here to smell that flower again. To start over. And more importantly I knew I had to let Chloe have a life."

"But she moved here too?" asked Jessie.

Madeline nodded. "Yes, in May. She was working for the college, but budget cuts resulted in her losing her job. It seemed practical for her to come here until she could find employment. Plus, she had joined the BRSC, and this area was the perfect training ground."

"BRSC?"

"There is a group—extreme sports nuts, I call them— that have made up their own take on a triathlon. Instead of swimming, cycling, and running, they are taking to the mountains for biking, running, and survivalist camping, BRSC, over a three-day, two-night duration. This year's event will be in September, starting from Estes Park in the Rocky Mountain National Park. The race starts on the night of the full moon with a bike ride to a campsite checkpoint, then a run the following day to a designated area where the participants camp overnight, run back to the checkpoint where they left their bikes and return to the finish line. The clothes on their backs and water are the only supplies allowed."

"People voluntarily sign up for this? And isn't September in the high mountains of Colorado a little late for a just-the-shirt-on-your-back camping?"

Madeline nodded. "The gamble on the weather is part of the challenge."

"Could it be she's in full-on training mode now? Could she have decided to camp out last night?"

"Possibly," Madeline drew the word out. "But I think she would have told me, or at least called me, if she decided to stay out all night. She's very . . . conscientious."

"She has a cell phone, I assume? You've tried calling her?"

"Yes, but it goes straight to voicemail. And now I've left so many messages her mailbox is full."

"As a single mother myself, I understand your concern, but as an officer of the court and one who's fiscally responsible to the voters, if I call out search-and-rescue and then find your daughter's just out 'training,' it would be a hard sell to the commissioners to foot the bill.

They may come back to you for reimbursement."

"I don't care how much it costs. I just want the reassurance my Chloe is okay."

"All right." Jessie sat back in her chair. "I'll make some calls to get a search started. Do you happen to have any idea the route she took?"

"I'm not sure. She talks about FS 222 being the most challenging."

The vibration of the sheriff's cell phone caused Jessie to jump. She glanced at the screen. "Excuse me, I have to take this." Jessie swiveled her chair away from Madeline and answered: "I'm busy. I'll call you later."

"Wait. We've got a problem."

"Go on."

"I can't find my gun."

"What?"

"Mama, the gun I had with me last night isn't in the RZR."

CHAPTER 6

Tuesday evening

TROY GRINNED as he shut the back hatch of the Jeep on two weeks' worth of groceries. The sheriff's "friendly advice" to stay off the mountain had been like an engraved invitation for him to go against authority. And it felt good. Really good.

AccuWeather had forecast rain with possible overnight lows in the 30s in the higher elevations. He crept up the main street, keeping an eye on the speedometer to stay under the speed limit. He didn't want another run-in with the oh-so-friendly locals. He did, however, have one stop to make before turning right at the end of the street.

"Welcome, young fella," Vince greeted Troy as he walked through the open door of Butler's Sporting Goods.

Troy glanced toward the back of the darkened store. "Looks like I caught you at closing. What time do you open in the morning?"

"I've got time if you've got money." Vince chuckled. "Are you looking for something in particular?"

"A fishing license, sir," Troy said handing over his driver's license for the second time today.

"Texas. You're a long way from home. You plan on fishing around here?"

"Yes, sir. Up on Pewter Creek Mountain."

"Been back in the states long?"

"That obvious?"

Vince grinned. "Thanks for your service."

"You serve?"

"Uncle Sam didn't want me." Touching his chest, Vince said, "Bad ticker."

Vince tapped the computer mouse. "Wake up, slacker." Vince hunted and pecked out the information on the keyboard. "Damn computers," he growled. "Wish I was going fishing myself. You might warn those brookies that Vince Humphreys has got two years to retirement, and then they'd better look out. Say, I've got a secret honey hole I don't mind sharing with you. It's a little tough to get to, off Forest Service Road 222, but it's well worth it. Need anything else before I close up?"

"Maybe look at your coats. Don't have much of a need for one where I'm from. But the weather forecast here sounds like it might get chilly."

A deep chuckle rumbled from Vince's chest. "Nothing better than a chilly sunrise in the mountains. Can't stand the heat myself," he said, walking down the aisle and stopping to flip lights on. While Troy picked up a few other supplies, including a camo jacket, Vince returned to the front register and drew a map to his secret fishing spot.

Troy dropped a box of Sour Patch Kids on the counter to add to his purchases. Vince screwed up his face and asked, "How the devil can you eat those things?"

"My buddy got me hooked on them. They're an acquired taste."

"Here's my map. I'm not much of an artist, so maybe I'd better explain my chicken scratches." Vince took a "Re-elect Sheriff Butler" pen off the counter and pointed at the map. "You are here," chuckling as he pointed to the square with an X. "The road splits at the end of the street, and you'll take a right onto County Road 37. Locals just refer to it as Mountain Road. Down the road on the left you'll see a three-foot turquoise seahorse perched on a giant seashell. That's Clara Brunner's mailbox. That Clara," Vince said, grinning. "She likes to live up to her name of Crazy Clara. Crazy like a fox, that old girl is.

"Anyway, past her drive is a sign for Nickel

Campground and Trailhead. After the campground on the left is a big parking area, Iron Trailhead, and the end of the county road. Lots of trails shoot off from there. Every year it seems the Forest Service scrapes in another road and sticks a trailhead sign up.

"You'll see the sign for FS 222. That two-track takes you clear through to meet up with FS 186. I've marked Berry Draw. It's a nice place to camp and close to the creek. And here is my honey hole," Vince tapped another X. "A rockslide back in the '80s changed the course of Pewter Creek. People call the slide area Big Rumble. Kind of a goofy name, but I suppose it did make quite a big rumble when the rocks started sliding down the hill. Anyway, the creek pools up on the other side of the slide before it meanders down past Nickel Campground toward town. Picking a path over loose shale and boulders bigger than a VW isn't the safest. Hence the reason few folks fish it.

"I put my name and phone number on the map in case you get lost," he continued, giving Troy a wink, "and I have to take off work to come find you. There's surprisingly good cell service on the mountain. In fact, better than places here in town." Vince shook his head. "Technology, don't understand it."

"Only going to get worse," Troy grinned. "Thanks for staying open late for me, sir."

"Call me Vince. Sir just seems too stuffy."

The rumble of Zane's high-idling diesel cut into the

quiet of Main Street as he parked in front of the store. Vince shook hands with Troy and followed him to the doorway.

Troy finished stowing his sack on the passenger's seat and gave Zane a nod before climbing into the driver's side. Vince stood on the store steps and saluted Troy as the Jeep backed out. "Made a decent sale," he said, turning his attention to Zane. "Rest of the day as quiet as the clientele next door," Vince said, chuckling. "Never gets old."

"Yes, Vince, mortuary jokes do get old." Zane walked behind the counter and flipped a switch. Music blared, causing Vince to cringe. "I told you keep the music on. It reminds people we are open for business."

Vince tapped his watch. "Past six. Store's closed."

"Whatever. Who was that guy, anyway, somebody passing through?"

"Nope. Headed up the mountain for some camping and fishing." *Wish it were me*, Vince said to himself as he walked toward the back of the store to turn out the lights as Zane closed out the register. Vince stopped to straighten a gas can on an endcap display before walking into the office. Zane stood over the cash drawer, reading the register printout, an orange can of beer in his hand. Pointing at the beer, Vince said, "You might want to slow your intake of that. Never knew booze not to get people in trouble."

CHAPTER 7

Tuesday evening

Highland City, Colorado

ABREE WELLS was emotionally and physically drained as she parked in the garage next to her husband's Accord. Her car's clock glowed, showing the time as after six o'clock. She had promised to be home early tonight, but the mayor's office had suffered a shitstorm this afternoon—the mayor's extramarital escapades had been leaked with the election only four months away—and she, as the public relations officer, had to clean up the mess.

She kicked off her pumps inside the dark laundry room, her mind already in the kitchen thinking "breakfast for supper." Dan wasn't a big fan of the meal, but her husband of three years could always step up and help with domestic chores. *Now that was laughable!*

She hopscotched toward the kitchen, working to release her right big toe, which had pushed through her reinforced-toe panty hose. *There's twelve bucks down the drain!* Her knee slammed into something solid, and she nearly face-planted. "Son of a bitch." She groped for the light switch and snapped it on. The largest suitcase from their luggage set sat in the middle of the floor with the garment bag draped over it.

"Dan, what's going on?" Abree asked as she walked into their recently remodeled kitchen. The remodel had cost a small fortune and had resulted in their first major fight. Dan said it was a ridiculous amount to spend, but Abree held strong—"Ninety percent of the time I spend in here is cooking for you, I deserve to have it nice."

Dan sat at the island, arms laid flat on the granite countertop, shoulders slumped forward. In front of him was a glass half full of amber liquid with one floating ice cube.

"Dan?"

He slowly raised the glass, changed his mind about a drink, and set it back on the counter. "Abree, we need to talk."

"About?"

"Us."

"Us?"

"This," he gestured between them, "this isn't working."

Wrinkling her nose, "What's not working?"

Frustrated, he stood and blew out a breath. "I'm moving out."

Abree started to take a step forward and then changed directions, moving to the cabinet right of the sink, where she pulled down a glass. Noticing the shake of her hand, she set the glass down and turned to face her husband.

Dan took a healthy drink before saying, "We've just been going through the motions of a marriage since—"

"Don't you dare say it," Abree said as she stepped forward and gripped the edge of the island. "Don't you dare," she stormed. Tears moistened her eyes, and her voice dropped to a whisper, "You promised it didn't matter."

"It doesn't. Not really." He paused, then continued. "I took a job with the Attorney General's office."

"You left the law firm without even discussing it with me?"

"It came up suddenly, and I had to make a quick decision. It's kind of complicated."

Anger simmered just under the surface as Abree replied, "I'm a college graduate, I think I can handle complicated."

"Sarah's dad is running again unopposed for Attorney General, but he really doesn't want to serve four more years. Sarah and I met him for lunch the other day, and he proposed that I join his staff, he mentors me, and when he steps down early in his term, I'll fill the vacancy and then run in the next election."

"Attorney General? You never said you were interested in politics. If anything, you said you got enough political BS being married to me."

"I have talked about the good I could do if I was in a position of leadership. You just never hear me," Dan said, with a hint of sadness. "Sarah says . . ."

Sarah. Dan's pushy, petite assistant who spent more time with Dan than Abree did.

"Are you having an affair with Sarah?"

"See, this is what I'm talking about. You focus on a ridiculous thing like me having an affair with my assistant instead of my career, our future."

Abree circled the island and reached for Dan's hand, but he drew it away and let it hang loosely at his side. "Let's try counseling, take a vacation, I'll give you space, whatever you want," Abree fired ideas like a Gatling gun.

At every suggestion, Dan shook his head.

"Dan, please let's talk about this now," she pleaded.

Dan's really gone?

Their talk had turned to tears for Abree, stony silence for Dan. Then, overcome with frustration, she had gotten angry. Dan had, too. Hurtful insults were traded before he'd walked out.

Now Abree sat in the dark knowing she should eat something because the alcohol she had drunk on an empty stomach was making her feel sick. But she couldn't make her legs move to leave the couch. She fumbled with her cell phone to hit redial to the one person she could talk to about what was happening—her best friend, Chloe Granger. But she wasn't answering her cell phone and her voicemail box was full.

Probably out on a crazy bike ride.

In college, Chloe had persuaded Abree to join her on outdoor adventures—biking, hiking. For Chloe it was a passion. For Abree it meant she could pursue her passion, high-calorie meals—especially sweets—and keep the weight off. Then she and Dan had married and decided to start a family immediately. Six months went by without a pregnancy. "Maybe you're working out too much," Dan had said. So that ended her time spent with Chloe racing down dangerously steep inclines and struggling up the next hills. Chloe had protested at first that Dan was too controlling, but she came to understand her friend's desire to become a mother.

Abree maintained the same high-calorie diet, however, and soon put on ten pounds—followed by another and another and another. Still no baby. Dan politely suggested maybe if she lost weight, it would help her fertility issues. Abree had begun the yo-yo gain/loss struggle. But still no baby. Fertility testing had been the next step, and it had brought devastating news—"I'm sorry, Mrs. Wells, the

35

results are conclusive. You are sterile. But there are other options, of course."

Not for her, there weren't. She absolutely wouldn't entertain the idea of a surrogate, and while there was, of course, a need for adoptive parents, she knew an adopted child would be a constant reminder of her empty womb. Dan continually reassured her that not having children didn't matter to him, just like her size didn't matter.

But in the end, those things did matter. He hadn't pulled any punches in their yelling match before he walked out—his sights were set on running for governor in the future, and a slender wife and children at his side was what voters liked to see.

So now, alone in the dead-quiet house, Abree's eyelids drooped and she drifted off into a booze-induced sleep.

CHAPTER 8

MADELINE'S KNUCKLES blanched white from tightly gripping the steering wheel on the drive back to her small homestead outside of town. The interview with the sheriff had left her feeling confused. She didn't understand the near-badgering she'd gotten from Sheriff Butler, and why she'd been asked all those personal questions. It wasn't until the end of the interview that the sheriff had finally taken down any information about Chloe. She'd even waved away the photograph, hardly looking at it, saying she would let Madeline know if she needed it later.

Madeline parked in her driveway, praying her daughter would be home, but her despair deepened after she rushed through the front door to find a still-empty house.

The shadow of Pewter Creek Mountain settled over the ranch-style home. Madeline stepped from room to room and turned on lights, unable to stand the gloominess of the house. Waiting for the water to heat in the microwave for tea, she flipped on the two outside lamps. Then she sat on the back porch, facing the forest and cradling her untouched cup of tea in her hands. She peered into the darkness at the trail that Chloe should return on, headlamp bobbing. A whirlwind twisted its way through the pines, signaling the approaching storm and whipping up Madeline's worry.

I won't survive losing Chloe too.

Madeline held her cell phone and the landline portable in her lap. She checked the landline's dial tone. The cell screen showed full bars. She hit redial to Chloe's number and heard the now-familiar "the user's voicemail box is full."

Feeling restless, Madeline set the cold tea to reheat in the microwave and walked down the hall into Chloe's room. She pulled her daughter's pillow from the bed and hugged it, smelling the herbal scent of hair products. A framed picture of Chloe and her best friend from college, Abree Wells, caught Madeline's eye.

"Why didn't I think to call her?" she scolded herself, and she rushed into the kitchen to retrieve her address book with Abree's contact information. Maybe Chloe had shared something with her best friend that she couldn't or wouldn't with her mother.

"Hello," Abree answered, her speech thick and groggy.

"Abree, it's Madeline."

"Hi. What's up?"

Madeline's voice cracked. "It's Chloe. She's missing. Have you talked to her?"

"Missing. What do you mean missing? And no, I haven't heard from her," Abree shook her head to clear the fuzziness. "In fact, I've tried her all evening, but her voicemail box is full, and she doesn't respond to my texts."

Through bouts of weeping, Madeline relayed what she knew and then hung up with the promise to keep Abree updated.

CHAPTER 9

Tuesday evening

SHERIFF BUTLER WATCHED Madeline drive away before climbing into the sheriff's department Dodge pickup. By now it was close to seven, but it seemed later with the thick storm clouds hiding the sun. She dialed Zane's cell number, and he answered after the second ring. "Hello."

"Are you at home?"

"No. At the store."

"I'll stop and pick you up."

"Where are we going?"

Jessie disconnected without answering. She tapped Eldon's cell number only to hear *leave a message*. His landline rang with the busy signal. She tried both numbers again and got the same results. She smacked the steering wheel. "Come on, Eldon. Answer your damn phone."

A bleary-eyed Zane jumped into the passenger seat as his mother came to a rolling stop in the middle of the street, not bothering to pull into a parking spot. "Son, you smell like a brewery."

"I . . . I . . . just," Zane closed his mouth and leaned his head on the back of the seat.

"What gun did you have?"

"The Heym."

"What?" her voice went up an octave. "You're telling me...," Jessie paused, a vein in her forehead bulging as she began ticking items off on her fingers, starting with her thumb. "You took the gun engraved with the Butler store logo out to go shoot up the woods? The lock, stock and barrel custom-made Heym Model 88B double rifle that's worth no less than $12,000 and which will be the center of attention in two weeks to commemorate the store's 25th anniversary?"

Zane just nodded and turned to stare out the window. Jessie cranked the wheel hard left into a U-turn and gunned the powerful Dodge. "I thought we were going to go up and look for the gun," Zane said softly. The pickup bounced through a deserted construction site. Zane straightened in the seat and asked, "What are we doing here?"

"Picking up barricades. We've got to keep people off

that road and out of those woods until we find that gun. I'm closing FS 222."

"Ranger Randy won't be happy with you messing around on his turf," Zane said with a smirk.

"Like I care. He's been a pain in my ass since he took the district job. Regulation this, rule that." A gust of wind rocked the pickup. "Weather's moving in. We'll have to work fast."

After loading four ACade sawhorses and two six-foot reflective orange-and-white boards with Road Closed placards screwed onto them, they headed out of town, following the road that ran parallel to Pewter Creek. A light mist began to cover the windshield as the brown-and-white FS 222 sign came into view. "We'll put the barricades up and then look for the gun if the weather holds." Zane and Jessie worked silently, setting the barricade across the entrance to the two-track road.

Back inside the pickup, Jessie stomped on the gas pedal, sending the truck into a fishtail as they headed up FS 222. She alternated between gunning the motor on the straight stretches and stomping hard on the brakes in the curves. "Walk me through last night."

A slight whine in his voice, Zane asked, "Do I have to?"

Jessie clenched and unclenched her fingers around the steering wheel. "It's important. I need to know everything."

Zane sighed, the air puffing out his lips. "We'd had a

few beers at the store. When I got home, Mary Beth started ragging on me about coming home drunk again, so I jumped on the RZR and took off."

"Where did you go?"

"Back to the store. I wasn't planning on going anywhere else, just hang out and do some Internet surfing. But then I saw the gun in the display case, and I thought, what would it hurt to go shoot a few rounds?"

They exchanged grim looks, knowing what it had hurt.

"What did you do next?" Jessie asked.

"I hauled ass up the mountain stewing about Mary Beth's attitude. She didn't care I drank before we got married. Now she's all Bible-thumping and quoting verses. I stopped to take a leak on . . . I mean in Crazy Clara's driveway by her mailbox. I remember shooting at a squirrel, but it was dusk and hard to really see anything. Then I came on up here for the hairpin curves and the uphill grade on this road." Zane fell silent.

"Go on," Jessie prodded.

"It was pitch black by then. I had just drove into the first switchback when a doe with fawns ran across in front of me. I swerved to the edge of the road and grabbed the gun and started blasting away in the direction they went. I'd ran over something when I left the road but didn't pay any attention, I thought it was just a tree branch. There was metal-on-metal scraping when I tried to drive forward onto the road, so I backed up and got out to look. That's when I saw the mountain bike."

Jessie looked at her son. The front of his T-shirt was twisted in his balled-up fists.

"And the woman?"

"She staggered onto the road, her hand over her heart. Her mouth opening and closing like she was reciting the Pledge of Allegiance. Lots of blood. It was so shimmery in the headlights." A choking sob escaped Zane. "I don't know why, but I gunned the motor and . . ."

Jessie watched her son use the tail of his T-shirt to wipe his nose. "Then I ran away into the woods. I must have come back sometime in the night, because I woke up leaned against the RZR tire."

As they climbed higher, moisture built up on the windshield, blurring Jessie's view. She clicked the switch of the wipers to a continuous swipe. "And you took the gun when you went into the woods?"

"I don't remember. I must have."

"Which direction did you go?"

Shaking his head, he replied, "I don't remember."

Jessie slowed as an intersection came into view. She was relieved to see no vehicles in either direction as she turned a wide circle onto the well-traveled FS 186, pointing the nose of the pickup back down the road they'd just traveled. She jammed the truck into park and opened the door. The wind yanked it from her hand. "Dammit. Weather's moving in fast. Probably won't be able to look for the rifle."

Zane opened his door and walked to the back of the pickup. "I still see her. When I close my eyes. I still see her standing there."

Jessie wrestled to set up the barricade alone while Zane stood staring into the distance. She slammed the tailgate shut, and Zane jumped. Jessie took his arm and led him back to the open passenger door. "Get in, Zane. We need to leave now."

CHAPTER 10

Tuesday evening

TROY SLOWED as Clara Brunner's mailbox came into view. He crept by, smiling at the giant seahorse and seashell. His grandmother loved seashells. *Maybe I'll surprise her with one of those for Christmas.* He could just hear his granddad's opinion of replacing their John Deere tractor mailbox with aquatic creatures.

He turned at the sign that read Nickel Campground. Clouds had hidden the sun, causing the temperature to dip, and twilight would come early with the approaching storm. Troy thought back to Sheriff Butler's "friendly" advice. She was probably right that a person could lose their bearings easily in the unfamiliar woods; best to set up camp close to the road for tonight. Troy knew one thing—he wasn't spending another night in the cramped Jeep when he was surrounded by acres of untamed wilderness.

By the time he had his backcountry tent up, a light drizzle had begun to fall. He ate a cold meal and lay on top of the sleeping bag, listening to the rain patter as it bounced off the nylon tent. The noise reminded him of being hunkered down in a shelter during a sandstorm—a memory he quickly shut down. He crawled to the flap and opened it to welcome the cool wetness on his face. After a few deep breaths of the mountain air, he zipped the flap shut, climbed into his sleeping bag, and was asleep within minutes.

Two miles away as the crow flies from where Troy was camping, Clara Brunner sat bundled in her handmade quilt on the porch of her rustic cabin. Listening to the rain drops splatter on the roof, she closed her eyes and inhaled the woodsy fragrance while the wind rustled through tree leaves. *Psithurism is salubrious,* she thought, recalling naturalist author W.H. Hudson's words from his book *Birds and Man.* He described the sound of wind in the trees—"To lie or sit thus for an hour at a time listening to the wind is an experience worth going far to seek. It is very restorative. That is a mysterious voice which the forest has: it speaks to us, and somehow the life it expresses seems nearer, more intimate, than that of the sea."

She knew people called her Crazy Clara because of her lifestyle—living alone in a cabin with no modern conveniences—and because she used words like psithurism and salubrious. But at the age of seventy-one, she didn't care what people thought of her.

She was content with life, living in woods that provided everything she needed. Rich black soil grew an abundance of garden vegetables. Hidden in draws, bushes hung heavy with sweet, plump berries. Fish from the nearby stream and the deer she harvested each year gave her protein-rich meat. She wasn't tethered to mind-altering objects—television with its blah-blah-blah white noise, computer games with overstimulating graphics, cellular telephone calls' constant assault on attention.

Chatter from a squirrel in a nearby ponderosa caused her to reflect on the death of Rickey, her pet squirrel. She knew the law wouldn't do anything about her complaint. She imagined the sheriff and her deputy sitting around laughing, poking fun at that "crazy old woman."

But there had been an assault in her woods last night. And if the man returned, Clara would take matters into her own hands.

CHAPTER 11

Wednesday morning

THE BUZZ OF THE ALARM jolted Jessie awake from a deep sleep. She hadn't been able to shut her mind down the first half of the night, and then around 2:00 a.m. a thunderstorm stalled over the region, packing high winds and torrential rains. She had finally drifted off just as the eastern sky began to lighten.

While the coffee brewed, she dialed Eldon's land line. It still rang busy. She left a voice mail on his cell telling him to saddle the horses and meet her at the office. The ATVs would be next to useless on the rain-soaked trails, and they might even come across some roads washed out.

Her number-one priority—find the rifle before someone else did.

Jessie walked to the sink and rinsed her cup, tipping it upside down in the dish drainer. With a reluctant sigh, she returned to the table and dialed the phone.

"Moody Search and Rescue. Jake speaking."

"Jake. It's Sheriff Butler."

"Good morning, Jessie. Got another fisherman hiding from his wife? I'll never forget the look on Peter's face when we stormed into his camp and told him his wife had reported him missing. How's the campaigning going? Rumor has it, Mr. Sinclair might give you a run for your money."

Ignoring the jab, Jessie said, "I might have a situation over on the mountain. Young woman may be missing. Just thought I'd give you heads-up I might need some help."

"I've got a skeleton crew on call. Most guys are over at Estes training, but I can round up a few. I'll come right now to set up search logistics—I'll split my crew, some start from this side and others come with me. We can plan to meet somewhere on the mountain. Just name the rendezvous spot."

Jessie chewed her upper lip. The last thing she needed was Jake Moody shadowing her every step. "Hold off for now. She might not even be missing. Got to keep my budget in mind."

"Jessie, if you could see me, I'm weighing bottom line

versus a human life."

"Well, it's not your bottom that would have to take the bill to the commissioners and beg to get it paid." She pushed End to cut off his reply.

Knowing Chloe hadn't returned overnight, Jessie wouldn't have any choice but to go through the motions of launching a search party.

Jessie was relieved to see Eldon's county pickup in the lot, even if it was blocking in Geraldine's Subaru—a fact Jessie figured she'd hear about. A mud-splattered horse trailer was hooked to the equally muddy pickup. Maybe all the years of the sheriff's budget financing Eldon's horses would finally pay off.

Madeline Granger jumped to her feet and rushed Jessie at the door. Puffy, red-rimmed eyes with dark circles underneath were a telltale sign she hadn't slept. She spoke fast, her words jumbled together. "She hasn't come home."

"Now take a breath, Madeline. Last night's storm moved in early up top and got mighty nasty. She probably had sense enough to hole up for the night. Fog's still hanging over the mountain this morning, so visibility's poor up there."

"Forecast for clearing by nine, according to AccuWeather," Geraldine inserted herself into the conversation, waving her cell phone.

Eldon walked in from the back to join the group, carrying two cups of coffee—the star badge emblem black against the white of the cup. His jaws mashed a wad of spearmint gum that did little to mask the heavy odor of alcohol.

Jessie accepted a cup with a nod and said, "Madeline, you need to go home and stay there in case Chloe comes back to the house. And you need to try and get some rest." She paused and took a drink before saying, "Mother to mother, I can't imagine what you are going through. Just know we are here for you and doing everything we can."

Madeline glanced from face to face. "What about a search and rescue team?"

Ignoring Madeline's question, Jessie turned to Eldon and asked, "Horses saddled?" He lifted his chin in a quick nod. Taking a step closer to Madeline and touching her arm, Jessie said, "The heavy rains from last night may cause some problems. Could be some rockslides." She put a hand under Madeline's elbow and ushered her out the door.

Geraldine returned to her desk, the air whooshing from her chair cushion when she sat down. "Madeline was waiting when I got here this morning. When I heard the news Chloe hadn't come home, I went ahead and called Ray Samson. He and Bella are on their way."

Jessie walked over to Geraldine's desk, picked up the metal nameplate, and ran her index finger across the black script.

"What are you doing?" Geraldine asked.

"Just checking to see if your nameplate reads sheriff instead of administrative assistant, since *you* called Ray and his very expensive search and rescue hound, Bella."

Geraldine crossed her arms over her ample bosom. The staring match broke when Jessie turned away, retreating to her office. She locked the door behind her. Unclipping her cell phone from its holder, she scrolled through her contact list. "Ray. Sheriff Butler here. Hope I caught you before you're too far down the road. We're going to have to cancel Bella for today. Conditions aren't safe." Jessie listened before replying, "Yeah, I understand time is important in a search, and I know Bella is an amazing hound. But I can't risk you or her getting hurt. Search area is riddled with potential rockslides."

Next, she sent a text to Jake Moody: "Woman still missing. Got search team coverage on this side. Rendezvous with your team at Granite Trailhead."

CHAPTER 12

Wednesday morning

TROY CRAWLED out of the tent onto ground made soggy by the overnight storm. He stood, stretched his six-foot-two frame, and faced the sun, which was quickly burning off the patchy fog. It had been his first full night's sleep in weeks without a nightmare; he smiled a full toothy grin.

He walked to the Jeep, his hiking boots leaving waffle patterns in the soft ground. A blue jay scolded him from among the thick pine boughs, and Troy answered back with, "Morning, Mr. Jay."

Troy was glad he had spent the extra coin on the top-of-the-line tent. The wind had rocked it during the night, but it had stayed put and was bone-dry inside. The outside held a beading of moisture, but he decided to break camp and move closer to Vince's favorite fishing spot off FS 222. He'd set up camp there, and the sun would dry his gear by nightfall.

All packed up, Troy drove slowly along the softened road bed. The Jeep's aggressive tires kicked up gravel; the pinging of rock on metal was loud inside the Jeep. He slowed to bounce over a wash that cut across the road; frothy water was rushing through the deep gash. He rounded the next curve and nearly crashed into a fallen tree limb. The heavy scent of pine filled the air as he lugged the debris to the edge of the road.

The farther the Jeep climbed, the softer the road became. Ahead was the Iron Trailhead turnoff that led to a large parking area. A sign posted on the right read End Winter Maintenance. He stopped the Jeep next to a black-and-yellow sign that warned of snowmobile crossing. Troy compared Vince's crudely drawn map with the one provided with his camping permit and made the decision to park in the turnaround. He'd go the rest of the way on foot.

He swung the loaded pack—it was light compared with what he was used to carrying—onto his back. From his jeans pocket, he brought out a compass to double-check his direction. He rubbed the engraved initials, **TAR.** The compass had been a gift to Trace Alan Richards from his granddad, given in a private moment shared before Trace shipped out to serve his country. On the long plane ride to Kabul, Afghanistan, Troy and Trace became friends and were soon dubbed the Double-Trouble Ts. *"Trouble just seems to find us,"* Trace had joked with their commanding officer when they returned from that disastrous patrol, the white gauze bandage above Trace's right eye soaked with blood. Troy's eyes had kept straying to the field-dressed stump where Trace's right leg should have been. *He'll have a hell of a time ever driving the Jeep he loves again,* Troy had thought as he stood beside the stretcher with his friend and watched the helicopter touch down. Trace had shifted the IV bag on his chest and dug into his camo shirt pocket. With a smirk on his face, he flipped Troy the compass, *"For you, buddy, to keep you moving forward in the right direction."*

Troy pulled his thoughts back to the present. "You're right, Trace. It's time I did move forward with my life." He took one last look at the compass before adjusting his pack and stepping out northward. As he climbed higher in the thinning air, his lungs protested, forcing him to stop. *Gone soft,* he thought as his legs quivered. Just seven months ago he'd been in the best shape of his life. But that was before Trace's alcohol-slurred phone call. *If I hadn't stopped to get him coffee, he'd still be alive.* He shook his head, driving the memory away. His counselor had warned that there was no easy fix, that you need to learn to recognize the triggers to help cope and deal with it.

* * *

Jessie walked into the front office to find it empty except for Geraldine. "Eldon's in the pickup waiting for you," she said. "Smells like he crawled into a bottle last night."

Jessie ignored Geraldine and walked past her desk toward the door.

"You going to check that weapon out?" Geraldine asked, pointing at the rifle Jessie carried. "Procedure manual says—"

Jessie held her hand up to stop Geraldine from launching into a recitation, verbatim, of the manual. "I know the rules, you know the rules. So just check the damn gun out to me. I've got better things to do than bureaucratic bullshit."

Jessie could smell the tang of fresh horse manure as she passed the trailer and crossed to the passenger side of the pickup. She opened the club cab door and laid the rifle across the seat, frowning at the greasy burger wrappers and french-fry cartons littering the floorboard. Eldon's cowboy hat was parked on the dash and his head was leaned back against the seat, eyes closed. He squirmed to sit up and rubbed his fleshy face with both hands.

The silence was heavy in the cab as they drove through town. The horses jostled to find footing as the pickup and trailer climbed up the mountain. Eldon cut a corner close, and the trailer slid off the shoulder into the mud.

"Better put it in four-wheel drive." Jessie said.

"You want to drive?" he snapped.

Jessie waved away an answer. "The creek was running fast past my house this morning. Must have gotten more rain up top."

"Besides the weather report, you got anything to tell me?" Eldon questioned. "Like what the hell you're planning on doing with Jake and his crew? And what is going to happen when Bella finds the body?"

"I canceled the dog. Used unsafe conditions with rockslides as an excuse. And I told Jake to start their search from other side and meet us at Granite Trailhead."

"Shit. Granite Trailhead. You plan on riding all the way over there? That's over five miles from here over pretty rough country. And there's no cell service in that area."

"I picked it because there's no phone service. And we're not going to Granite. I was just buying us some time. We'll park at Iron Trailhead."

"Time for what?"

"If you'd answered your phone yesterday, you would know we've got a problem. Zane's gun is missing." Jessie turned in her seat to face Eldon. "And don't you ever go radio silent on me again."

Eldon shifted his weight in the seat and glanced out the window at the red flag raised on Clara Brunner's mailbox as they passed. "What about the girl's mother?"

"Madeline Granger will be easy to contain. I

interrogated her yesterday, and she's got no family except Chloe and hasn't made friends here. We'll just make sure to keep her isolated at home waiting."

Eldon grunted and pointed out the windshield. "Got fresh tracks up ahead."

Jessie pulled herself forward, gripping the dashboard. "Looks narrow, like a Jeep with oversized tires."

They followed the tracks into the large graveled parking area. "Texas plates," Eldon said. "Somebody's a long way from home."

"Not far enough," Jessie breathed the words out.

Shortly after leaving his Jeep, Troy's path had crossed a well-traveled deer trail, and he followed cloven-hoof tracks until they intersected with a two-track road. Looking at the map, he confirmed he was on FS 222. Vince's fishing spot should be up ahead several miles and to the right. The black dirt path was slippery, and he had just stepped off it when an unfamiliar sound echoed in the quiet forest. The sound came again, closer this time, and Troy recognized it as a horse clearing its nostrils. An even-closer snort was followed by curt instructions: "Hands up. Keep 'em high."

The sheriff kicked her mount past her partner to face Troy and leveled the rifle barrel at his chest. "On your knees."

Eldon swung off his horse and knocked Troy down

before he could comply with the sheriff's request. He jerked Troy's backpack off and threw it out of reach as the sheriff slid the rifle into the scabbard. "Well, Mr. Troy Edwards, you should have heeded my friendly advice to stay off my mountain."

CHAPTER 13

Wednesday afternoon

ABREE KNEW it was a rash decision, but what was done was done. Shortly after 8:00 a.m. she had gone into the mayor's office and asked for emergency family leave, explaining that Chloe was like a sister to her. The mayor had sputtered, red-faced: "Are you out of your fucking mind, Abree? I'm fighting for my life in this election, and you want to go play nursemaid? It's all hands-on deck here — a unified front."

Abree had tried to count to ten before answering, but at two she'd said, "I quit," turned, and left the mayor screaming after her.

Now she crept down a tree-lined lane, hoping she had followed Madeline's directions to the correct turnoff. She expected to see cars parked at odd angles, people spilling out of the house onto the lawn. Maybe even a news van. That was the way it was on television when someone was missing—people rallied around the family. But when the house came into view, she saw no one. In fact, the place looked deserted.

Maybe everyone is at the search and rescue command post.

Abree ran up the sidewalk and was about to knock when the door flew open and Madeline fell into her arms.

"What do you mean there isn't a command post?" Abree asked after Madeline recovered enough to speak.

"Well, we're not really sure Chloe is even missing. She might just be training for that stupid marathon. The sheriff . . . well, it's expensive to call in the search and rescue team. I said I didn't care how much."

"Why was the sheriff discussing money when a person's life may be at stake?"

Madeline threw up her hands. "It's all so confusing and overwhelming. I'm just not good at stuff like this. Kent always took care of everything, and after he was gone Chloe stepped up."

"Sheriff Butler sounds like he's a real dipshit."

"She. Sheriff Butler is a woman."

"Well, then She Sheriff Butler is a real dipshit. I'm going to the sheriff's office to get some answers."

"She said I should stay here in case Chloe comes home

or calls."

Abree rolled her eyes. "Leave a note, take your cell phone with you. Let's go."

On the drive to town, Abree asked, "Madeline, where are your friends?"

Madeline looked down at her clenched fists. "I haven't really made any yet. I'm nearly as much of a hermit as Crazy Clara."

"Crazy Clara?"

"She's an older woman who lives in a rustic cabin on Pewter Creek Mountain. She's a little eccentric, so people started calling her Crazy Clara. Chloe befriended her because of all her time spent on the mountain biking and hiking. Clara calls the woods her backyard. We've sort of adopted her as much as she lets us. I take her baked goods. Chloe helps with the chores around the cabin—chopping wood, hauling water."

Abree parked her car beside Geraldine's Subaru. "Sounds just like Chloe—helping others. So, let's go in and help her."

Within an hour of walking into the office, Abree was out the door with missing person flyers to distribute throughout the town. Geraldine had turned her computer over to Abree and started making phone calls to her Methodist women's group. The reception area began to fill with card tables overflowing with food. A large coffee pot perked away, filling the small room with the rich aroma of fresh-ground beans. A group of women surrounded Madeline, taking turns hugging her and urging her to eat something.

Abree went from business to business along the street and was met with surprise, concern, and offers to join in the search. She had only one flyer left when she walked into the sporting goods store.

Zane was alone, sitting at the computer in the small office surfing the website "Asian Women Looking for Love." He reached for a beer—not taking his eyes off the surgically enhanced woman on the screen—and knocked it over, spilling it across the pile of unpaid bills cluttering the actual desktop. Ignoring the sodden mass, Zane was still ogling the woman when he heard a voice over the blaring music. "Hello, anyone here?"

Zane slammed the laptop shut and bolted out of the office.

"Oh, there you are," Abree said.

Zane grabbed a box of Junior Mints and tossed a few into his mouth. Mumbling around the candy, he asked, "How can I help you?"

Abree launched into her practiced speech about the local woman gone missing. "We are gathering at the sheriff's office to help with the search. May I put this flyer up at the cash register?"

"Sure thing," Zane said as he stepped forward to take the flyer. He glanced at the face smiling off the page and staggered backward, toppling a cardboard display stand and sending cans of insect repellent clattering across the floor. Regaining his footing, he said, "Oops, tripped."

Abree bent down and picked up a stray can. "I'll help you set the display back up."

"Don't bother. I . . . I," Zane stuttered, his body language ushering her to the door and onto the sidewalk. He pinballed off the doorway and along the wall back into the office, where he grabbed his cell phone. His call went to voicemail, and he stammered into the phone. "They're putting up missing person flyers and gathering at your office."

Abree eavesdropped as she wove her way through the crowd that was milling around in the parking lot of the sheriff's office. ". . . do everything we can . . . praying for safe return." *Now I need to have a come-to-Jesus meeting with She Sheriff!*

Madeline, seeing Abree walk through the door, broke away from a group of ladies and gathered her into a hug. "Thank you so much for this," she indicated the room full of people. Abree blinked away tears, warmed by the feeling that she was making a difference by helping someone who appreciated it.

"Is the sheriff here?" Abree asked, gratefully accepting a cup of coffee offered by a sun-tanned woman wearing a Western snap-front shirt.

Madeline frowned. "No," she said. "She and Deputy Johnson are searching the mountain on horseback."

The *whoop* of a siren set the roomful of people rushing out the door. A path cleared as the pickup and horse trailer pulled into the no-parking zone.

The driver's door flew open, and Jessie climbed out. Eldon emerged from the back seat, shotgun looped across his forearm. Sheriff Butler, hand hovering above her unsnapped holster, stood back as Troy swung his legs around and jumped out, hands cuffed behind his back. The sheriff, speaking loudly, said, "Folks, step back. Give us room."

A jumble of questions went up—"Where's Chloe? . . . Who's that guy? . . . Is she dead?" Zane stepped forward and addressed the gathering, "You heard the sheriff. Move back."

Eldon swaggered forward in front of Troy, the sheriff bringing up the rear. Madeline rushed from the crowd and stepped into the sheriff's path. "Where's Chloe?"

"Madeline, I'll talk to you later."

Abree stepped around Madeline and barreled into Troy, crashing them both hard to the ground and screaming in his face, "What have you done with my best friend?"

It took a few minutes to disentangle Abree and Troy. Eldon roughly pushed Troy toward the steps. Abree, pulling Madeline along, kept in stride with the sheriff, firing question after question until Jessie finally said,

"Lady, shut the hell up." A string of people followed closely behind, eager not to miss the action.

"Eldon, stick him in the cell and meet me in my office. Geraldine, clear these people out of here and lock the door. I need an update on just what the hell is going on here!"

Geraldine joined Jessie in her office. A worried look on her face, she took the chair opposite her boss. "Jake Moody called to say they were starting down Gold Gulch Road, but their pickup radio is on the fritz, so they'll probably be out of communication from here on out. They said they'd see you at Granite Trailhead. I don't know what's keeping Ray. He should have been here by now."

"You having a tea party out front?" Jessie asked. "And who's the woman who should be playing tackle for the Broncos?"

Eldon joined the women and perched on the edge of his desk, his muddy cowboy boot swinging. Little dirt balls pinged into the side of his green metal trash can. Geraldine gave him a motherly "stop that" look and kept talking. "Abree Wells. She's Chloe's best friend, and I guess things were moving too slow for her big-city personality. She distributed some flyers, and the news spread." Shrugging her shoulders, she said, "You know how small towns work—we rally behind our own."

Jessie moved to look out the window and cringed at the sight of a KOLD news van in the parking lot. The telephone began ringing at the same time as there was a loud banging on the front door.

"Go answer the phone, Geraldine," Jessie said. "And tell the reporters no news conference until tomorrow, so they might as well go chase their own tails."

Eldon slid off his desk and took Geraldine's vacated chair. "What a fucking circus! Got a plan?" he tipped his head toward where Troy was locked in the cell. "Got to either charge him or let him go."

"Thanks, Einstein, for that bit of information."

"Why didn't you just tell him to get off the mountain? Seems you complicated matters bringing him in."

Blowing out her breath, she said, "Because he isn't very good at following directions. But depending on how things play out, he might be just what we need. Bring me his pack and the envelope out of my saddle bag. Then go take care of the horses, get something to eat, and come back." Mimicking Geraldine, Jessie said, "Procedure manual says no prisoner may be left unattended while in the custody of the Pewter Creek Sheriff's Department." She ran her fingers through her short, dishwater-blonde hair until it stood on end. "I need to go visit with Madeline and set some ground rules with Little Miss Troublemaker. I'll relieve you at midnight."

Eldon snorted. "Ain't nothing little about her. But seriously," he said as he shuffled toward the door. "This whole mess got trouble written all over it."

"Eldon," Jessie said, softening her tone, "everything

will work out okay. Don't worry. I've got your back, just like you've got mine. Right?"

He opened his mouth to speak but closed it as Zane pushed into the room.

"Wow! Just like a page out of a Western, right, buddy?" Zane said, punching Eldon in the shoulder. "The sheriff and his deputy bringing in the desperado at gunpoint!"

Eldon ignored Zane and walked past him out of the room. Jessie motioned for Zane to close the door. He pushed it, not noticing the latch didn't catch. The door swung back open a few inches.

Jessie's chair made a creaking sound as she adjusted her weight. "What were you doing out there with all those people?"

"I came to talk to you. You didn't answer your phone when I called to tell you they're putting up missing person flyers and organizing a search party. Besides, I'm a leader in the community. I'm expected to be front and center where the action is." Zane plopped down in Eldon's chair and set his can of Mountain Dew on the desk. "The dude you brought in was in the store. Made a nice sale off him."

"When was this?"

"Just before closing last night. He was leaving just as I got there."

Jessie remained quiet, tapping her index finger on her upper lip.

"What are you thinking?"

"If he didn't go up on the mountain until late, it means he didn't have time to do much snooping around since the storm moved in."

Zane jumped to his feet and began bouncing on his toes, fake dribbling as he crushed the drink can and shot it at Eldon's basket. The can bounced off the rim, and Mountain Dew dribbled onto a clump of dirt. "But you took care of everything, didn't you? Up on the mountain? It shouldn't matter if anyone goes up there."

The door swung open, and Geraldine stepped through. She gave Zane a puzzled look, then shifted her eyes to the sticky mud on the floor. Addressing her boss, she said, "I'm taking off."

Jessie nodded and followed Geraldine out, stopping where she could see the front office was empty. "Zane, I'm serious when I say you need to keep a low profile until this all blows over. And watch what you say. You never know when people are listening."

"Yeah, yeah. You forget we own this town?"

"I'm saying just be careful. Maybe you should take off with Mary Beth this weekend when she goes to stay at her parents."

"No can do. School board meeting. Executive session. Mary Beth's cousin Laramie got herself into some hot water, and I need to remind some of the school board members how much the Butler family does for this community. Do you want the details of the sexy English teacher's dalliance with the quarterback?"

Jessie grimaced and shook her head. "I'll pass. Just keep your head down and your mouth shut."

CHAPTER 14

Wednesday night

TROY'S REQUEST to make a telephone call had been met with stony silence as Eldon pushed him into a room, past a metal table and two folding chairs toward a tiny cell in the corner. *Probably just as well,* thought Troy. He didn't know who he would call. He sat down on the bed, the plastic crinkle of the mattress sounding loud in the small space.

Stay calm, he thought. "Easier said than done," he said aloud. He took a deep breath and thought back to the mountain and what had happened after he'd been told to reach for the sky.

The smell of the horse's sweat mixed with that of the deputy. Sheriff Butler kept the firearm trained at Troy's chest. "Deputy Johnson is going to pat you down, so don't do anything stupid." Eldon jerked hard on Troy's arm to pull him up from the ground then kicked his legs apart. Eldon did a quick pat-down and began to empty the contents of Troy's pockets into a pile on the ground.

"Here, put that stuff in this envelope." The sheriff waved a manila envelope, causing her horse to dance sideways away from the flapping paper.

"What about his pack?"

"Tie it on the back of your saddle."

"Daisy ain't going to go for that. Sugar Drop won't either. She'll buck your ass off."

Through clenched teeth, Jessie said, "Then put it back on Troy and cuff him in the front."

The deputy clambered back onto his sorrel. Troy fought to keep his footing on the slippery trail at the pace set by the two mounted law enforcement officers. The temperature had climbed into the 70s by the time they reached the parking area, and Troy's shirt was soaked underneath the new heavy jacket he wore. Jessie stood, shotgun looped over her forearm, while Eldon trailered the horses. "Throw his pack in the pickup bed. I'll drive."

Troy, seated behind Jessie, studied her face in the rearview mirror. Her eyes remained intent on the road in front of her, never meeting his gaze. Eldon squirmed in the seat beside Troy, trying to get his girth comfortable in the restricted area. Troy watched the shotgun come within grabbing distance and knew, even handcuffed, he could get the upper hand over Barney and Gomer. But then *what?*

Eldon buzzed the window down, and Troy welcomed the circulation of fresh air. In the straight stretch ahead, Troy noticed a woman retrieving a brown-wrapped package from the seashell mailbox. "Crazy old bat!" Eldon hollered out the window as they passed by her.

The small parking lot in front of the sheriff's office was jammed with cars. People milled around in small groups in front of the building, and the door to the office stood open.

From the questions he heard hurled at the sheriff, Troy determined a young woman was missing. The screeching woman who had tackled him evidently thought he was the number-one suspect in her disappearance.

And now he was locked in a cell, left to sweat it out until the powers that be decided what to do with him.

There was only one car parked in front of the two-car garage at the Granger residence. The sheriff noted it wasn't local and ran the plate—Daniel and Abree Wells.

AKA Abree the Troublemaker.

Madeline answered the door. Abree hovered close behind her.

Jessie stepped into the entryway. "It's been a long day, and I could sure use a cup of coffee if you wouldn't mind."

Madeline began measuring grounds into a filter basket while Abree filled the maker with water. "Sheriff Butler,"

Madeline said, "I don't think you have been formally introduced to Chloe's best friend. This is Abree Wells."

"Pleasure to meet you. It was good of you to come and be with Madeline at such a difficult time."

Abree stood, arms crossed defiantly across her chest. "The man you brought in—what is he saying? I don't understand why you didn't have a local search party out. Everyone I visited with said they would have gladly searched all last night, regardless of the weather conditions. They didn't even know Chloe was missing before I sounded the alarm. What about the search and rescue team? And the search dog? It seems to me that you have dropped the ball." Abree's voice rang loudly in the small kitchen.

The sheriff held up her hand. "Ms. Wells, I know you are worried about your friend, but unless you have actually conducted a missing persons search, I don't think you're qualified to tell me I'm not doing my job." Accepting the cup of coffee from Madeline, the sheriff continued. "I can assure you both that everything in my power is being done to locate Chloe. I have no control over the weather, which has been quite a detriment to our search efforts.

"As far as the person we brought in, I'm not at liberty to discuss that at this time. Tomorrow will start early, so I'll be taking off. Thanks, Madeline," the sheriff lifted her untouched cup of coffee, then set it on the kitchen table and made her exit.

* * *

As Jessie drove toward home, she longed to crawl into her king-sized bed and pull the covers over her head. Maybe this was all just a nightmare. Instead, she exchanged the county pickup for the RZR, which had been parked out of sight in her garage since Tuesday and headed back up the mountain.

Jessie didn't care much for the RZR. She had been partial to her side-by-side, but it had long ago been sold to cover gambling debts. *His* gambling debts. If only they could have all been paid off by simply selling an all-terrain vehicle. But true to what the pamphlet said, gambling was an addiction, one that was hard to control.

And Rodney Butler had had no control. No matter how many times she'd heard "I'll never gamble again" from her husband, she knew he'd never quit until everything they owned was gone. He'd proved it when he lost Butler's Sporting Goods Store to real estate developer Curtis Winslow in a card game. Jessie had no choice but to enter an extortion-level deal with Winslow to keep up the appearance that the Butlers still owned the store. As she suspected, real estate developers were a greedy lot. Though Curtis professed to be a silent partner, he was anything but silent when his payment was late.

Shortly after that fateful card game, allegations of inappropriate use of government funds had begun swirling around Sheriff Rodney. The Attorney General launched an investigation, and after a stressful six months, it was announced—the morning before opening day of elk season—that Rodney was cleared of any misconduct.

To celebrate, Rodney and Jessie planned a hunt. But the night before they were to leave, Jessie developed a stomach virus. At her urging, Rodney left the house on that frosty October morning for a solo hunt on Pewter Creek Mountain. He had not returned by nightfall, and the alarm was sounded.

Every able-bodied person headed to the mountain and joined the search. Others gathered at the Butler home to support Jessie and young Zane, and they got the news just after midnight—Rodney Butler had been found shot to death. It was eventually ruled an accidental shooting, a stray bullet from an unidentified hunter.

At the urging of the community, Jessie agreed to step into Rodney's boots and become the first female sheriff of Pewter Creek. Three generations of Butler men had pinned gold stars to their chests and prospered from the control, not to mention the perks that went with the title of Pewter Creek Sheriff.

Sixteen years later, Jessie Butler still wore the badge, and she planned to keep it that way. Whatever it took to protect her only child.

Jessie's thoughts were bleak as the ATV growled its way up the mountain. Zane's casual drinking had grown into a full-blown problem—an addiction—a genetic flaw he'd inherited from his father.

By the time Jessie reached Iron Trailhead, the August sun had set. She parked on the gravel skirt in front of the barrier blocking FS 222. Rainwater still pooled underneath the barricade. Her size-seven cowboy boots sank into the mud as she walked up to it and attached a printed sheet, sleeved in a plastic protector. Her flashlight beam swept across the two-track ahead, reflecting the gleam of mud. Jessie tapped her phone to check the time; she had three hours before she had to relieve Eldon. Because of the muddy trail conditions, she would need every bit of those three hours to do what needed to be done.

CHAPTER 15

Early hours of Thursday morning

JESSIE TAPPED HER CELL PHONE SCREEN again to check the time.

3:33. *Half evil,* Jessie thought, trying to remember where she'd become acquainted with the term. Probably some tattoo on a bad-ass biker's "most wanted" poster.

She rolled her neck, working out the stress kinks. She was operating on very little shut-eye over the past few days, and it was beginning to take a toll. She picked up the Re-elect Sheriff Butler pen off her desk and rolled it between her hands. An audible sigh escaped as she thought about the upcoming election. She dropped the pen back in the cupholder and rested her forehead down on top of her desk.

Jessie had run unopposed the past four terms for the office of Sheriff of Cobalt County. But now Wayne Sinclair, the police chief of neighboring Copperville, had thrown his hat in the ring. It was making Jessie's comfortable, predictable life a little less comfortable and a whole lot less predictable.

Fighting heavy eyelids, Jessie walked to the small break room and started a fresh pot of coffee. *The Cobalt County News* lay on the counter next to the tray of cups. Jessie skimmed the front-page headlines and flipped the paper open. She scanned obituaries on page two, bypassed the third page of statewide news and was brought wide awake by page four — the smiling face of Wayne Sinclair in a full-color ad asking, *What has your current sheriff done for you lately?* Underneath was a bulleted list of his accomplishments.

Wayne was considered an outsider by most of the folks in the county because he was not a third-generation Cobalt Countian. But he had made a name for himself in Copperville by cleaning up the drug issue that had plagued the town. He'd busted two meth labs and shut down an opioid distribution center. Working closely with the city fathers, he had secured grants to improve ambulance service within the city limits, brought the DARE program into the schools, and had a door-to-door campaign educating seniors about scammers. His campaign promised that, if elected, he'd bring bigger and better improvements, county-wide.

Jessie grabbed the paper, wadded it up, and shoved it into the used coffee grounds at the bottom of the metal trash can. *Screw you, Mr. Wayne Sinclair.* She pulled a clean cup from the tray and began pouring the steaming coffee. The sound of her cell phone ringing startled her, and the hot liquid splattered across her hand. The ringtone increased in loudness with each chime, an annoying setting she didn't know how to disable.

"Jessie, it's Jake Moody," a gasping voice came across the line.

"Jake, what's wrong? Are you okay?"

"It's bad," the leader of the search team said.

Jessie held her breath, wondering what the impact of his next few words would be for her.

Jake continued, sounding less breathy. "The road gave way underneath the pickup, and we crashed down into a ravine. Sterling and Wade have some serious injuries. My arm's broken, but I was able to walk out to get cell service."

"What can I do to help?"

"Nothing for right now. I've got EMS on the way. And a tow truck. The wife's borrowed a Suburban, and she's on her way. Got to go. I see headlights coming, and I'm off the road up on a hill."

* * *

Troy had remained awake throughout the night, sure that if he slept in the small, enclosed space, his haunting nightmare would return. He couldn't afford to lose control. In the past, when people had told him what he'd said and done in the throes of the nightmare, he'd accused them of making it up. But the sleep study video had not lied.

As the light began to increase through the tiny cell window, Troy hollered out, "Hey, sheriff! I want to talk." Troy waited a few more minutes, and yelled, "Sheriff Butler, I need to tell you something."

Time ticked by before the door to the room swung open. "I'm listening," the sheriff said, standing in front of the cell door.

"I'm hungry."

"Hungry?"

"Yes, ma'am. Hungry. And thirsty."

"That's what you want to talk about—food? Not why you were brought off the mountain in handcuffs and spent the night in jail?"

"Well, maybe we could talk about that over breakfast."

"You sure act like a guy with nothing to lose." She stepped forward, eyes narrowing. "Am I right that you don't have anything to lose?"

Troy stood silent and unmoving in the center of the cell. The sheriff shook her head. "Oh, what the hell. I'll order breakfast, and we'll have a little chat."

* * *

Jessie returned to the room with two cups of coffee. Eldon followed and dropped a white plastic sack on the metal table. Jessie stood to the side as Eldon opened the cell door and handcuffed Troy.

"Are these really necessary?" Troy asked. "I promise I'll be good."

"Just following the procedure manual," Jessie responded.

Jessie finished her breakfast first, as Troy found it awkward to eat with his hands cuffed. "Thanks for breakfast," he said as he placed his plastic spoon and folded napkin in the empty Styrofoam container before closing the lid. "That sure hit the spot." Troy waited for a response from the sheriff, who just continued to watch him. "Am I being charged with something? Just saying. I haven't been given my one phone call."

"You watch too many cop shows."

"And my Miranda rights?" questioned Troy.

"Did you see that on an episode of *Law and Order?* Mr. Edwards, this is real-life cops and robbers." She paused before adding, "And murderers."

"Is this where I stop talking and ask for a lawyer?"

The sheriff stood and lunged across the table, shoving Troy hard in the chest, knocking him backwards. Troy and his chair crashed to the floor, his head hitting the concrete with a *thunk*. The door flew open, and Eldon stood in the doorway, pistol drawn. "Everything okay?"

The sheriff stood over the dazed Troy. "Sure thing, deputy. Mr. Edwards tipped his chair a wee bit too far back and had an unfortunate accident. He'll probably need a little more cell time to fully recover. I'll be home if you need me."

CHAPTER 16

Thursday morning

"ABREE! ABREE!" Madeline called out. "Look at this."

Abree threw back the bedcovers and leaped to her feet. Her world went dizzy, and she quickly bent at the waist and put her head between her knees. Her heart thumped loudly in her ears as she slowly stood up, focusing on Madeline coming through the bedroom door. Waving her cell phone, Madeline said, "It's from Chloe."

Abree focused on the screen and quickly scanned the message, then reread it aloud: "Mom, I'm so sorry that I must have worried you. Just need some down time. I'll be out of cell service. Going to hang with a friend. Don't worry. I'm fine. Love you."

Tears of relief streamed down Madeline's face as she retrieved the cell from Abree and hugged it to her chest. "I'm so relieved. I was so scared I'd never see my little girl again. So many times, the missing person story ends in heartache. You know they find them but . . ." she trailed off. "And sometimes they're never found, leaving the family to wonder forever. I couldn't bear to lose her."

Abree hugged Madeline. "It's such a relief. We'd better let the sheriff know. Do you want me to make the call?"

"No, it's one call I'll be happy to make."

Troy stood at Geraldine's desk, waiting for Eldon to return with his pack and the envelope containing his personal effects. He rubbed the sore spot on the back of his head. *Stereotypical small-town sheriff's department.* He had been cuffed and stuffed, not charged with anything, never questioned about the missing woman, and now he was being released without any explanation.

A breeze blew through the open front door, ruffling the papers on Geraldine's desk. A commotion in the parking lot drew Troy's attention. He walked to the doorway to see people circled around the sheriff, a news crew among them. A red Accord drove into the parking lot, and Sheriff Butler walked to the car.

Geraldine joined Troy. "I see Madeline and Abree have arrived for the sheriff's photo opp." Scorn dripped from her voice. "At least it's a happy ending."

Outside, Sheriff Butler cleared her throat and held her hand up to quiet the crowd. "I am happy to report that Chloe Granger is safe. She, in fact, was never missing, just out of cell range. Madeline," Jessie surprised the woman by pulling her into a hug, making sure the camera captured both their smiling faces. Letting her go, the sheriff addressed the crowd. "On behalf of Chloe's family and friends, and the sheriff's department of Pewter Creek, we want to thank everyone for their prayers and assistance during this very stressful time."

Troy watched the expression on Abree's face when the sheriff hugged Madeline. *Not a big Sheriff Butler fan.* He remembered Abree's tackle. *Guess the same goes for me.*

Madeline said something to the sheriff, and Madeline and Abree weaved their way through the cheering crowd, returned to the red car, and drove away. The ringing phone brought Geraldine back to her desk, and Troy turned when she exclaimed, "Oh, my God."

Geraldine rushed Jessie as she came in from the parking lot. "Wreck on 111. Fatalities. Blazer T-boned a fuel truck. HP on site. Hazmat on their way."

The sheriff stopped close to Troy. Not taking her eyes from him, she said, "Geraldine, cancel the search teams. Tell dispatch I'm on my way. And Mr. Troy Edwards, I guess I don't have to tell you that you got a free pass this time. Might not be so lucky in the future." The subtle scent of cherry almond lotion lingered after Jessie walked away.

Geraldine returned to her desk, saying, "I don't know what's keeping Eldon. Sometimes that boy can't find his . . . well, you know, with two hands." She consulted a sheet of paper in front of her, picked up the telephone, and dialed. Troy listened to Geraldine's one-sided conversation: "Ray, the missing woman has been found. You have our address to send your invoice to. You won't see your check until next month, the commissioners just met last week." There was a long pause and then Geraldine said, her voice louder, "I don't understand. You're telling me the sheriff called and canceled Bella? That you never even left home?" Ray responded, and Geraldine ended the call with, "Well, I guess that's that."

Eldon shuffled into the room, dragging Troy's backpack behind him. He tossed it at Troy's feet with a thud. He dumped the contents of the manila envelope onto Geraldine's desk. "You need to sign this discharge sheet. And guess I don't have to tell you to get the hell out of town. Your Jeep was towed to the Conoco station." Eldon chuckled and started for the outside door. "Wouldn't want to have to pay that bill."

Geraldine stood up from her desk. "Eldon, bad wreck on 111. You better . . ." She trailed off, glaring at the retreating back of the deputy who didn't stop to acknowledge her.

Troy noticed immediately that Trace's compass was not among the items spread across Geraldine's desk.

Eldon had gotten a little rough with Troy when he had emptied his pockets, first tossing things on the ground and later stuffing them into a manila envelope—which he'd handed off to the sheriff. Troy remembered hearing the envelope crinkle as the sheriff crammed it into her saddlebag. Maybe Eldon hadn't picked it up. Or Troy had missed putting it in his jeans pocket earlier, but he didn't think so.

"Is anything wrong, Mr. Edwards?" Geraldine asked.

Smiling at her, Troy said, "No, ma'am. Nothing." But he was thinking, *I'm sure the hell not leaving Pewter Creek without that compass in my possession.*

Troy stood in front of the counter at the Conoco station, drinking coffee as black as used oil and reading the bulletin-board postings. A campaign poster for Wayne Sinclair was front and center. He turned toward the sound of glass rattling in a slammed door. A short block of a man dressed in greasy coveralls clomped toward him. Troy noticed the stitched *"Ralph"* on the left front pocket was beginning to unravel. "Thought you'd be one of them darkies 'cause of your Texas plates."

"No, sir. Scandinavian ancestry."

Ralph rolled a cigar stub from one corner of his mouth to the other. "Only take cash," he said thrusting a paper toward Troy. "ATM over yonder, if you need it."

Eldon had been right about the towing fee. Troy

pulled five crisp hundred-dollar bills from his wallet and watched as Ralph fingered each one and then held them to the light for closer inspection. He tossed the keys to Troy. "Out back."

Troy's plan was to return to the mountain and begin the search for the compass, but Eldon's muddy county pickup sat idling in the Conoco parking lot. Troy had no choice but to pretend he was leaving the area. After topping off his fuel tank, he pulled out of the station and drove by the Thank You for Visiting sign, keeping under the posted 45 miles-per-hour speed limit. Eldon had pulled out, too, and he tailed Troy until he exited onto the state highway, which would take him out of Colorado toward Kansas. *They not only don't want me in their county, they don't even want me in their state.*

Madeline had been totally exhausted when she and Abree returned home from the news conference. The adrenaline of keeping vigil for Chloe was ebbing, and she was having trouble putting one foot in front of the other. Abree persuaded her to eat some casserole that Geraldine had sent home with them earlier, before she went down the hall to her bedroom.

As Abree washed up the dishes, her mind whirled with questions about Chloe's strange actions. And about what she should do about her own future. She retreated to the rocking chair on the back porch with a glass of iced tea.

The ring of her cell phone startled her, and she hurried to retrieve it from her pocket, hoping it would be Chloe.

"Where are you?"

"Hello to you, too, Dan."

"I called your office to talk to you, and they said you quit your job. And you're not at the house."

Abree gave him the abridged events of the past few days, ending with, "Not that it's any of your business anymore. You've moved on."

After a long pause, she heard Dan's breath rush through the phone. "About that. I've decided I'm not right for the attorney general's office."

"And I need to know this why?" Abree asked, unable to keep the sarcasm from her voice.

"I want us to try to make our marriage work. Let's take a vacation. Maybe Hawaii."

Abree paused long enough that Dan asked, "Are you still on the line?"

"I am. It's just . . . I don't know. I need a few days to think."

"I'll give you space. Just come home. You said Chloe's not missing, and Madeline will be fine. They don't need you, but I do."

But what do I need? Abree thought.

CHAPTER 17

Friday morning

ABREE WOKE the next morning with a headache, her mind still reeling with questions. Should she go back to Dan and try to make their marriage work? What did she want to do with the rest of her life, and did she even want Dan to be a part of it?

She couldn't shake the hurt and confusion centered around Chloe's actions. Why hadn't she shared her feelings with her best friend? They texted almost daily—silly things like "word of the day" or the link to a blast-from-the-past song. The latest was Blondie's "Heart of Glass." But they shared personal details too. And who was this person she was off with now—a secret lover?

Madeline was standing over the stove, and the aroma of French toast filled the tiny kitchen. "Just in time," she said, looking well-rested as she plated the slices and set the two plates on the table with a bowl of mixed fruit and two full coffee cups. "What are your plans for today?"

"Nothing special. How about you?"

"Joyce, one of the women from the Methodist Church, asked me to join the women's group for their monthly luncheon." Fidgeting with her napkin, she said, "I actually feel like going."

"You definitely should. This is a wonderful little town with so many caring people. There was so much support for you after we told them Chloe was missing. I'm still miffed, though, with the way She Sheriff handled it."

"I'm sure Sheriff Butler did what she thought was best," Madeline said. "About the luncheon, I'm sure it would be fine if you came with me today."

"Thanks, but I have some heavy thinking to do." She moved a bite of toast through the dark syrup shimmering on the plate. "Actually, Dan and I are having problems." *And I want answers from Chloe,* she thought.

"Oh, I'm sorry to hear that. Marriage definitely takes work. Please let me know if I can help in any way."

"I will. And thanks for letting me stay here until I figure some things out."

"Take all the time you need."

* * *

With Madeline gone, Abree wandered into Chloe's room. Everything in the room reminded Abree of her friend and brought back memories they had shared, making Chloe's actions even more hurtful.

On Chloe's desk was a Forest Service trails map. Trails were marked in different-colored markers with detailed notes concerning each one in a notebook next to the map. *That's Chloe—organized to the point of being over-the-top irritating.* Abree could imagine Chloe picking up a half dozen of these trail maps to squirrel away in her pocket, backpack, and car. Abree scanned through the pages, stopping at the sheet that read "Nickel Campground and Trailhead." It had five red stars across the top of the page and a note: "big-ass thinking rock." FS 222 was highlighted in neon yellow on the trails map, but a search through the notebook showed no corresponding notes about the trail.

Taking the map with her, she jotted a note for Madeline telling her she was driving to Nickel Campground.

Troy had slowly rolled through the deserted streets of Pewter Creek just before three a.m. Friday, hoping Sheriff Butler and Deputy Johnson were home snug in their beds. After passing the now-familiar turquoise seahorse mailbox and the sign pointing to Nickel Campground, he had driven off-road to hide the Jeep behind a stand of pines. *No use advertising I'm up here.*

Just after sunrise he covered the ground to the Iron Trailhead parking area quickly, and his search for the compass came up empty. Frustrated, he had returned to the Jeep and was now staring into the cooler at his meal choices. Snapping the lid shut, he gathered his fishing gear and headed the half mile to Pewter Creek.

So far, the score was trout two, Troy zero. He had nearly gotten the last one to the bank before it escaped, taunting him with a disappearing flip of its tail. He was nearing a bend in the creek when the sound of a loud splash caused him to stop. Smiling, he thought, *I've got the feeling I'm going to catch me a big one.* The sound came again, and he stepped from a heavy grove of aspen to get a clear view of the water. Abree was perched precariously on a large rock looking down into the water below. She stood up and tossed a stone and then curled her arms around herself. A loud sob carried on the still air. A few minutes later, she stumbled as she tried to take a step and wipe at her eyes at the same time.

Better stick around and keep an eye on her, Troy thought as he worked his way into a position to make sure she made it back down the trail safely. He watched as Abree, head down and concentrating on where to step on the slippery trail, was startled by a noise to her right. A squirrel darted across her path causing her to trip. Her foot caught on an exposed tree root, and she fell forward, her left knee slamming into a jagged rock. She cried out, rolled onto her backside and pulled her jogging suit pant leg up. Blood gushed from the wound.

Troy crashed through the timber onto the trail and ran toward Abree. At the sight of him, she screamed, "Stay away from me. I have mace."

"I'm not going to hurt you. You need help," he said as he slowed to a walk and pointed at her knee.

"I can manage."

"At least let me bandage it," he said sliding the backpack off his shoulder.

"No!" Abree struggled to get to her feet, falling back in defeat. The movement caused the gash to open further, blood spurting onto the trail. "Oh, my God. I'm going to be sick," she said, turning her head as the French toast of this morning made its appearance. Troy handed her a bottle of water. "Thanks. And why the hell did you scare me and make me fall?"

Troy's lip twitched. "From my vantage point, I think it was a squirrel that sent you ass over teakettle."

"You mean you were watching . . . stalking me?" she asked, trying unsuccessfully to crab walk backwards.

"Relax. I'm harmless. Besides earlier you looked like you were upset, and I didn't want to leave you alone. But I didn't want to intrude, either." Pointing to her knee, he said, "That cut needs stitches."

"What? Are you a doctor?"

"No, but I play one on TV."

"Give me a break." Despite trying to act annoyed, a smile curved her lips.

After Troy dressed her knee, he offered her his hand and pulled her to a standing position. "I'll just carry you to your car. You definitely need to stay off that knee."

"You can't carry me. I'm . . . well, I'm. . ."

"Big-boned?" Troy said. Giving Abree no time to argue, he swung his backpack on and shouldered her into a fireman's carry. "I'm Troy. Troy Edwards. I didn't catch your name."

"Because I never threw it," Abree said, a giggle escaping.

CHAPTER 18

Friday morning

GERALDINE JUMPED UP and followed her boss into her office. Waving a fistful of pink messages, Geraldine sat down in the chair across from Jessie and pulled it up close to the desk. "You're letting important things fall through the cracks. Some of these people have called two and three times. Do I need to remind you the election is coming up? Wayne is out making friends in this county."

"Been a little busy, you know. Missing woman. Wreck on 111."

"I can't reach Eldon AGAIN. There's a report of cattle out at Winston's Junction."

Geraldine pushed back the chair and stood up, hands akimbo, waiting for a reply. When the sheriff just met her gaze without comment, Geraldine turned on her heel and stomped off, calling back, "I'm going to get the mail."

The sheriff pawed through the stack of messages, pausing to read the upcoming candidate forum dates and a request from Wayne Sinclair for a debate. *Screw you! And the jackass you rode in on!*

Her cell phone skittered across her desk, vibrating with a call. She recognized the number immediately and would have rather signed up for a root canal than answer. But not answering would come with consequences, so she hit Accept. "My payment's late." Three words and a *beep* signal. The call had ended.

Jessie stood with Zane and watched out the store's window as Vince pushed through the glass door into Rosie's Diner. "Did that Edwards guy hightail it out of town after his recent accommodations?" Zane asked, his hand shaky as he grabbed for the nearly empty sixteen-ounce Mountain Dew bottle.

"As far as I know. Hopefully he's not a slow learner, but some jarheads are—all brawn, no brain. Let's talk in the office," Zane's mother said as she grabbed a packet of peanut M&Ms from the candy counter.

"Got to hit the can first," Zane said.

Jessie wrinkled her nose at the telltale smell of beer as

she passed the trash can just inside the office doorway. She shook her head at Zane's cluttered desk. "I raised you better than this," she said aloud as she straightened a pile of papers that teetered close to the desk's edge. An envelope with a red past-due notice caught her eye.

Zane walked through the door waving his hand in the air. "Closed that wing of the building." He stooped in front of the mini fridge coming up with another bottle of Mountain Dew. The crack of the seal followed by the hiss of carbonation sounded loud in the small office.

"How's business?" Jessie asked.

Zane took a healthy gulp and replied, "Busy."

"Too busy to pay bills?" she motioned to the red-stamped envelope. "And I haven't seen my check for this month."

Zane began alternating tapping the toes of his sneakers: right, left, right, left. "Oh, I'm a little behind on bookwork. You know, all the little day-to-day BS of running a small business. I'll deposit it this afternoon."

Jessie studied her son's face, noting small lines that hadn't been there six months ago. She looked into his bloodshot eyes. "We haven't found the missing rifle yet. We need to get up there before the weekenders start poking around. Who's scheduled to work today?"

"Vince is coming in at eleven. Jason's got a baby-daddy appointment today since Amanda's due next month."

"Get over to Rosie's and tell Vince you need him to

come in early. Then pick me up at the house in the RZR."

While Sheriff Butler waited for Zane to return, she made a mental list of things to do. She was going to have to step up her election campaigning. And if the store was running in the red, that brought a series of problems she would be left to deal with. But the number-one priority was to find the missing rifle.

She moved out onto the store steps just as Zane and Vince pushed through the café door. Jessie had never been a Vince Humphreys fan, but Zane had argued in favor of his hiring—he had a good rapport with the old farts, and the bottom line needed their moldy money.

"Morning, Sheriff Butler," Vince said tipping his cap, its Butler Sporting Goods logo smudged with dirt.

"Vince. Looks like you could use a clean cap," she said as she straightened her shoulders and brushed past him down the steps.

"Just got this one broke in." Vince took off his cap and rubbed at the smudge on the "B" in a circle. "Say, Zane, I noticed the Heym isn't in the display case. Didn't you put an ad in the paper inviting people to come in and see it? A sort of pre-anniversary celebration tease?"

"Yeah, I did. I . . . ah took the rifle home the other night to show a buddy who was coming to the house. Just forgot to bring it back."

"What do you want me to tell the hordes of people fighting their way into the store to see it?" Vince chuckled.

"No reason for that kind of sarcasm. How many sales have you made this month?"

Vince spread his legs wide to face off against his boss. "You insinuating I'm not pulling my weight?"

"Listen, Vince. We've got to work as a team for the good of the store. Just remember what a struggle learning the POS system was for you. Technology is changing the face of retail. This day and age, Internet sales are where it's at. I'm working on launching our website sales link. Just think about whether you're up to the challenge." Zane grabbed a handful of candy bars on his way past the register. "Got to run."

Vince clicked the mind-numbing music off and stood in the window behind the register, musing whether it was worth the headache to stick it out two more years with his little jerk of a boss. It seemed those brookies were calling his name more and more these days.

Jessie made good time on the sun-dried road as she and Zane headed up the mountain to search for the missing gun. They had passed Clara's mailbox and the Nickel Campground sign when Zane said, "Ah, Mom? I need to come clean with you."

Jessie slowed and pulled the ATV onto the shoulder of the road. "What?"

"I did take the gun with me when I ran into the woods. And I remember shooting at some noises in the bushes. But I really don't remember the direction I took from the road, and I don't remember what I did with the gun afterwards."

Jessie got out of the machine and walked off the road into the knee-high grass and low brush. She bent at the waist, fighting dizziness. *What if there had been more than one rider in the woods that night?* She stood up slowly, shaking away the thought. As she turned back toward the road, a shiny reflection caught her eye. "What the hell?" She crashed forward, followed closely by Zane.

"Isn't that Troy Edwards's Jeep?" Zane asked as the pair walked up to the partially concealed vehicle.

Through clenched teeth, Jessie said, "It certainly is. And tomorrow I'll take care of Mr. Troy Edwards once and for all. But for right now, we'll search until we find the gun or until it gets dark. Whichever comes first."

CHAPTER 19

Friday late afternoon

IT WAS NEARLY FOUR O'CLOCK by the time the discharge nurse watched Abree swallow the pain pill and cautioned her not to drive. Addressing Troy, Abree said, "I'll call Madeline to come get me, and she can drive you back up the mountain."

"How about I drive you to Madeline's, and we can make a plan from there?"

Troy stole a glance at Abree's profile as they drove to the Grangers' place. Her eyes were closed, her head leaned back against the seat. Wisps of her sandy-brown hair had escaped the scrunchie and framed her round face. Her left hand moved to rub the area above her injured knee. The diamonds in her wedding band sparkled in the sunshine. *I wonder where hubby is,* Troy thought, returning his gaze to the road ahead.

Madeline rushed off the porch as Troy carried Abree up the sidewalk. "You," she said with alarm, backing away.

"Madeline, it's okay," Abree said. "This is Troy Edwards."

"Ma'am." Troy nodded. Madeline held the door for Troy, and he set Abree down on the sofa.

Madeline hurried to sit beside her, taking her hand. "What happened?"

Embarrassment reddened her face. "I tripped and hit my knee on a sharp rock and had to go to the ER and get stitches. Troy . . . I guess you could say—"

"Was in the right place at the right time." Troy finished her sentence.

"Oh," Madeline said.

"Do you think you could drive him back up on the mountain?" Abree asked.

Before Madeline could respond, there was a rap on the door. "Who in the world?"

"That will probably be my ride," Troy said. Madeline returned from the door, Vince walking behind her. After introductions were made, Troy said to Abree, "When you were getting stitched up, I called Vince for a ride."

Cap in hand, Vince said, "Glad you called, Troy. I

never miss an opportunity to go up on the mountain. And glad, Abree, you are okay. Say, something sure smells good in here."

Madeline's face flushed. "It's just a pot roast, but I insist the two of you stay for supper," she said. "It's the least we can do to thank you." Troy gathered a protesting Abree in his arms again, and they trailed Vince and Madeline into the kitchen.

Madeline began apologizing. "It's nothing fancy. We really haven't had a decent meal in days with everything going on. I just thought it would do both of us good to have a home-cooked, sit-down meal. What may I get everyone to drink?" she asked as she took two more plates from the cupboard.

Vince spoke up. "I wouldn't turn down a cup of coffee."

Their conversation centered around the events of the past few days, with Madeline doing most of the talking. Abree's comment of "stupid She Sheriff" caused Vince to chuckle and nod in agreement. Troy concentrated on the plate of food in front of him.

The meal finished with an apple crisp, a scoop of ice cream semi-melted over each helping. "I can't take credit for the crisp," Madeline said. "I was a guest at the Methodist ladies' luncheon, and one of the women insisted I bring it home."

"Verlene?" asked Vince.

"Yes, how did you know?"

"She's pretty famous for her potluck crisp. I've tried to weasel the recipe out of her, but no go."

"You bake?" Madeline asked, surprise in her voice.

Vince nodded, "I'm chief cook and bottle washer at my house, being single. I've even been known to wash a window or two."

"I hate to break up this Susie Homemaker moment," Troy said, "but I think Abree needs to get some rest. Looks like her pain pill might be getting the best of her."

Abree looked around at the mention of her name, eyelids drooping and a goofy smile on her face.

"Madeline seems nice," Troy said, adjusting himself in the pickup seat.

"Abree seems nice," Vince countered.

"Touché."

"She was darn lucky you happened along," Vince said slowing the pickup for a deer that darted across the headlights.

"Why do I think there is more behind that statement you aren't saying?"

"Just coffee gossip. Some still think Chloe might have met with foul play. That maybe the guy's still out there." Vince's hazel eyes held Troy's for a second before he looked back to the road.

"Because?"

"Anybody can send a message from a phone. If you

didn't have your phone password-protected or if I knew your password, I could send a text to anyone on your contact list."

"I'm impressed, Mr. Geriatric. You know cell phone buzz words—text, contact list, password-protect."

Vince chuckled. "Don't let the snow on the mountain fool you. But seriously, I think something smells like a three-day old brookie left out in the sun. You got camp set up?"

"The entire Pewter Creek Mountain is my camp," Troy replied.

"So, drop you anywhere?"

"Works for me. I sure appreciate you driving me back up here. Can I ask another favor?"

"Sure thing."

"Look in on Abree tomorrow. And Madeline."

"My pleasure," Vince said, chuckling.

After Vince drove away, Troy used his penlight to work his way back to his Jeep. The caffeine from three cups of coffee left him too keyed up to settle in for the night. He found a log to sit on, and in the stillness, he listened to the growl of Vince's pickup fade away. After a few more minutes, the sound of an ATV crackled in the distance.

I wonder who else is on the mountain tonight?

Troy thought over the earlier conversation with Vince.

Is the town right to keep questioning Chloe's disappearance? He had caught an uncomfortable vibe from Vince and didn't like feeling like Vince might think he had something to do with the missing woman.

Troy did agree with Vince, though, that something smelled fishy. His money was on Sheriff Jessie Butler being involved because of the conversation between Geraldine and the owner of the search dog. Why would the sheriff cancel the hound before getting news that Chloe was safe? And where was his missing compass? Troy was almost certain it had gone into the envelope given to the sheriff. The whole incarceration stank to high heaven of small-town sheriff in charge—nothing was done by the book. It wouldn't be the first time in history that a cover-up and planted evidence led to a falsely accused man serving life for murder.

CHAPTER 20

Saturday morning

THE NIGHT HAD BEEN ANOTHER SLEEPLESS ONE for Jessie. It was after ten before Zane dropped her off from another fruitless search. A glass of wine and hot bath hadn't had their normal effect of helping her to shut her mind down. She had continued to cycle through her list of problems—the upcoming election, possible fallout from the financial problems at the store, Zane's drinking, the missing rifle, and now Troy Edwards. For whatever reason, he wasn't going away, so it was time to learn who she was up against. She'd stop at the office later and run his name.

In the meantime, Jessie spun the dial on her home safe. She reached in and pulled out the round compass from the top shelf, turning it over to run her thumb across the **TAR** engraved on the back before slipping it into her jeans pocket. Maybe Troy's background would shed some light on the significance of the initials. Jessie picked up the purple cell phone with the bedazzled C and debated turning it on and sending Madeline another text. She decided against it—"Chloe" had said she'd be out of cell range. Jessie put it back in the safe next to the two untraceable 9mm handguns. Every cop she knew had a burner piece for that one day, that one time, when there was no other choice. Jessie traded her service pistol for the untraceable Glock before locking the safe.

Abree's phone rang and rang until she finally crawled up from her drug-induced sleep. Forgetting her injured knee, she rolled over to retrieve the device, crying out as pain shot through her bandaged knee.

"What?" she answered.

"Abree," Dan said. "Are you on your way home?"

"No. What time is it?"

"Ten o'clock. Why haven't you left to come home?"

"I fell yesterday and split my kneecap open, so I'm on some pretty heavy-duty painkillers."

"Have you thought about us?"

Abree looked up to see Madeline standing in the

doorway waving a pair of crutches. "Dan, now isn't a good time. I've got to go." She hung up without a good-bye.

"I didn't mean to interrupt," Madeline said.

"You didn't."

"Vince brought these by for you this morning." Blushing, she added, "He just left."

"Vince?" Abree said, raising her right eyebrow.

"Oh, Abree. I feel kind of silly. I only met him last night, but it seems like we've known each other for years. We have so much in common. He stopped to check on you and brought you these crutches. Want to take them for a test drive? I have fresh coffee cake."

Vince chuckled to himself as he drove into the store's rear parking lot remembering his two-hour visit with Madeline this morning. "Vince, you old coot. You're acting like a love-struck teenager."

He was still feeling euphoric when he walked around the corner of the block and found Zane's RZR parked in front of the store. Shaking his head, he thought, *never know what toy he'll be driving next.*

Vince was surprised to see Clara Brunner peering into the front seat of the blue-and-white machine. "Good morning, Clara."

"Good morning to you, too, Vince."

Vince just plain liked Clara. And respected her too.

There'd been lots of speculation about what drove a single woman in her 60s into the hills ten years ago. Had she lost her family at the hands of drunk driver? Had she been the driver? Or, and Vince really got a chuckle from this rumor, the witness protection program? He didn't care, he didn't judge. Everyone has the right to live their life as they wish, if they don't do harm to others or themselves.

"Want to go for a spin? I'll warn you, this one is darn loud. It's got a souped-up custom muffler and sounds like an angry bumblebee."

"Is it yours?"

"Naw, it's the boss'. I've got an older one, a side-by-side. Let me help you in." Vince made sure Clara's seatbelt was buckled before taking off down the street. He watched with puzzlement as Clara cocked her head from side to side, listening to the noise coming from the engine. By the end of the ride, her white fuzz stood at attention, showing her pink scalp underneath. "So, are you sold on getting one? It would beat walking back and forth from town to the cabin. And it'd help with hauling things."

"Vince, what are you doing?" Zane asked leaping from the top step of the store to the sidewalk below. "I was about to report my RZR stolen."

"Just taking Clara for a spin," Vince said, giving Clara a hand out of the passenger side.

Zane, ignoring the woman completely, jumped behind

the wheel and called over his shoulder, "Going for lunch."

Vince turned back to bid farewell to Clara just in time to see her point her finger and thumb, gun style, at the retreating Zane and pull the trigger.

CHAPTER 21

Saturday morning

JESSIE COULDN'T REMEMBER the last time she'd been to Eldon's house. It sat next to the dilapidated barn and falling-down corrals on five acres he rented west of town. He had lived in the same house his entire life—first with his parents and two siblings, and later with his widowed mother. His older brother and sister had escaped the domineering grip of Mother Johnson.

Knee-high grass had grown around a faded red lawn mower, which sat in the middle of the yard like a lawn ornament. Mother Johnson's once-colorful perennial border across the front of the house was choked with weeds.

After following Troy out of town on Thursday, Eldon had returned to join Jessie to work the accident on Highway 111. It had been a grisly scene—parents deceased, fourteen-month-old twins in the backseat protected from physical harm by their car seats. The screech of the Jaws of Life saws blended with the cries from the inconsolable toddlers who were collected by child welfare services. Jessie had told Eldon to go home after he had helped the coroner load the mangled bodies of the mother and father.

Jessie stepped onto the porch. "We need to talk," she called through the tattered screen door. Eldon pushed the door wide to allow Jessie to pass by him into the house. She crossed over to the television remote and silenced *Rooster Cogburn*. Eldon sat at the kitchen table and watched Jessie clean the coffee carafe, fill it with water and start the Mr. Coffee. She leaned against the stained white sink. "I'm not sure what's going on with you, but I don't appreciate you not answering my calls. And what was with just not showing up for work yesterday? We need to keep a unified front. Business as usual."

"You tell me one thing about what we did the other morning that qualifies as 'business as usual,'" Eldon snarled, his voice hoarse. He stood and began to pace back and forth. "Jessie, we've done some questionable things in the past. And I've gone along with them. But this . . ." He stopped and leaned toward her, his face inches from hers. "Did you see Madeline's face? She thinks her daughter is coming home someday."

Jessie stared back at him, thinking hard. "Tell you what, Eldon," she said. "This has been a tough week. You go saddle the horses. I've got some lunch stuff in the pickup. We'll just take a ride on the mountain and have a picnic. Maybe we can spot the herd of elk, or maybe we'll find some vermin and rattle their cages."

Troy double-checked the supplies in his pack before locking the Jeep doors and snapping the carabiner keychain to the loop inside the backpack. His mood this morning was a mixture of frustration and curiosity, with a big helping of anger thrown in. He was frustrated because he hadn't found the compass yet, curious about Chloe's disappearance, and angry at the treatment from Sheriff Butler and her lackey. He especially didn't like feeling that Vince might think he had something to do with the missing young woman.

He shouldered the heavy pack, picked up the canvas bag of food supplies and took off walking with the intent of setting up a more permanent camp closer to Big Rumble and Vince's fishing hole. He soon reached the Road Closed barrier on FS 222. A slight breeze blew the plastic-sleeved sign warning "ROCKSLIDE AHEAD" that was duct-taped to the orange-and-white planks. He studied the surrounding ground and frowned, trying to figure out what wasn't quite right with the scene. He sat down in the shade of a pine tree, ate an energy bar, and downed a bottle of water before it dawned on him.

"Tracks!"

He circled the barrier and saw that the only tracks in the dried mud were small boot prints leading to and from the sign duct-taped to the barricade. If the barrier had been set in place the morning after the rainstorm, there would have been vehicle tracks and several sets of footprints.

"I wonder what secrets lie up this road?"

By the time Troy had walked two miles, he was sucking air. He definitely understood now why the trail was marked extreme. He stepped off the path, following a deer trail, and walked behind a group of berry bushes to relieve himself. As he turned to zip his jeans, he noticed something orange in the tall grass. He used a stick to flip the orange-and-black beer can onto the trail—Black Tooth Brewing Company out of Sheridan, Wyoming. *Wonder if Gramps has tried this brand out. Maybe I'll head to Wyoming to see family when I'm done with Colorado.*

Curious to see where the deer trail led, he followed it for several more yards when something shiny caught his eye—shell casings, 300 Win Mags. *Somebody up to no good,* he thought as he dug the casings out of the mud and pocketed them. Continuing down the damp path, he rounded a curve and spooked two spotted fawns away from a tan-colored heap in the grass. Troy could smell the sickly-sweet odor of decaying meat as he drew close. Flies buzzed around the doe's ripped hindquarters where animals had feasted. Troy held his breath as he bent over, inspecting the ragged hole in the belly. *Gut shot.*

"Son of a bitch." His grandfather had taught him to be a conscientious hunter—shoot to kill, not wound. He returned to the main two-track and consulted the map, deciding to work his way down the steep slope on the south side of the road to an area known as Berry Draw.

Satisfied with his camp setup, he returned to the main road and followed it over the summit and down the other side to where it intersected with FS 186. Another plastic sleeve was taped to the Road Closed placard warning of a rockslide down FS 222. "Yup, something is fishy for sure." The barricades were definitely staged to keep people off this road. But were they to hide evidence of high-power gunplay? Or a missing woman?

Jessie twisted in the pickup seat to reach the cooler in the back, retrieving Cokes for herself and Eldon. "Let's park at Iron Trailhead and ride down to Nickel Campground. We'll picnic by that big rock that overlooks the creek."

The pair rode in silence until the rock came into view. "Heating up out here," Eldon said, mopping his brow with a red kerchief. The smell of horse sweat filled the air as Jessie and Eldon stopped in the shade.

"How about you stay here and relax. Sugar Drop needs to be reminded she can ride away from another horse." She handed over her saddlebag. "Set up lunch. I won't be long," Jessie said as she touched her spurs to the belly of the buckskin.

She planned a circular ride of the area: search the north side of FS 222, cross over near the summit and weave her way back on the south along Pewter Creek down to the campground. With luck she would find the missing rifle, and she was sure she would run into Troy's camp somewhere along the way—maybe even Troy himself. She touched the unregistered gun in her holster. Jessie's anxiety grew as she skirted downed timber and scrubby thickets. So far she was zero for three—no rifle, no camp, and no Troy.

Sugar Drop lunged the last few feet up the steep incline onto FS 222, catching Jessie off guard and slamming her painfully into the saddle horn. She rubbed her midsection and squinted against the sun as she looked into the ravine below. Big Rumble sketched a giant V down the mountainside, its black rocks a contrast to multiple hues of green.

Uneasiness niggled Jessie. What if Troy was camping near the rockslide area? She knew Pewter Creek pooled on the other side, and the few who braved crossing the jumble of rocks had returned with monster trout.

Decision time.

Should she take the time to check the slide area? Had

the recent rains uncovered what needed to be left buried? If Troy was in the area, that would be a huge problem—one she would need to deal with ASAP. But on the other hand, if he hadn't gotten this far yet and happened to come across her tracks in the rain-softened earth, he was just the sort to be curious enough to follow them.

Jessie reined Sugar Drop off the road in the direction of the campground and clucked her tongue. She'd return to the mountain alone tonight in the cover of darkness to check around Big Rumble. As she and Sugar Drop neared Berry Draw, the gentle, playful sound of water tumbling over rock did little to calm Jessie. She was lost in thought when Sugar Drop shied, nearly dumping her off. The breeze had rustled a camo tent staked against a rock outcropping, spooking the horse.

"Whoa, girl," Jessie cooed, rubbing the horse's neck. She swung down, keeping both reins tight in her leather-gloved hand, and led the horse away from the campsite. After securing the reins around a tree branch, Jessie walked back to the camp. She poked around inside the tent and recognized Troy's recently purchased jacket.

Time to rattle his cage.

She slipped her knife from her jeans pocket and quickly got to work slashing the coat, sleeping bag, and tent to ribbons. She looked around the area and spotted his canvas food bag up in a nearby tree. She brought it back into the camp, destroying the food as she slung it all over the site.

A smile of satisfaction on her face, she swung up onto her mount. "Sugar Drop, let's go have a picnic. I've worked up quite an appetite."

Jessie dismounted beside Daisy, loosened the cinch, and looped Sugar Drop's bridle reins around a branch. Eldon was sitting, bourbon bottle within reach but his food untouched. He rummaged in the saddlebag and held out a peanut butter and jelly sandwich and an apple for her. Jessie walked over to stand by the creek and ate her sandwich, mesmerized by the moving water. She returned to sit beside Eldon and ate her apple, tossing the core at a chipmunk that darted from a rock crevice. "This is nice. Helps to take a person's mind off everything."

Eldon sucked his tongue against his teeth and nodded his head in agreement.

Jessie drained her water bottle. "After the election, let's come up here and elk hunt. Get away for a few days."

"Jessie, I want more than a few days with you. I've wanted that for a long time."

"Now just isn't the right time."

Eldon reached the bottle of Jim Beam and took a healthy drink. "It's never the right time. You always have some excuse—too soon after Rodney's death, overwhelmed with the job, wouldn't look right dating my deputy. I've told you more than once I'm willing to quit my job so we can be together, but you always come up with some crisis and beg me to stay on as your deputy. And it usually has to do with Zane. You need to let that boy grow up.

"Jessie, I need to make a change. This last week . . . well, let's just say I don't think I can do this kind of work any longer. And I'm drawing a line I won't cross anymore." Eldon rolled to his knees and pushed off the ground.

Jessie studied his retreating figure. Now she had to add her deputy's conscience to her list of worries.

Troy began a jog to retrace his steps back to his camp. His gut was telling him it was time to get off the mountain so he wouldn't get caught up here by Sheriff Butler again. Soon, though, Troy's oxygen-starved lungs and aching legs forced him to stop. He tipped his head back to drain his water bottle and noticed a couple of vultures circling across the ravine at Big Rumble. As he watched, the two were joined by another. It was probably another dead animal, but if it was another senseless kill, Troy intended to contact the game warden. The edge of the road was a sheer drop-off and looked too dangerous to climb down. Back-tracking down the road, he found an easier route and slid down the rocky path until the ground leveled out. The scavengers continued to circle, growing in numbers. Ahead was a recent path through a stand of willows. Judging from the distance between the strips of crushed greenery, Troy gauged it was an ATV track. The recent rains had matted the grass, swirling dirt over the top like something from an abstract painting.

Troy picked his way to stand at the base of the massive rock pile. The recent rain had washed silt and small rocks away, exposing large black stones glistening clean in the bright sunlight. The smell of carrion increased as he skirted around to the right, surprising a red-headed vulture. The large bird flapped and hopped its way away from the mouth of a deep crevice created by two large boulders. Troy's hiking boots gripped the slick rock as he scrambled to peer down into the shadowy darkness. "Damn." The body of a purple-clad woman was partially hidden beneath rocks and the mangled frame of a bike.

CHAPTER 22

Saturday afternoon

"I'M GOING STIR-CRAZY," Abree announced when Madeline brought lunch in and set it on the coffee table. "I know I've only been an invalid for a day, but it seems like *soooo* much longer."

The oven timer buzzed, and Madeline stopped before returning to the kitchen. "Why don't we take a drive after lunch? The banana bread will be cooled by then. We can take Clara some loaves and then stop at the store to do some shopping." Her complexion brightened. "Vince is coming for supper."

The crutches stowed across the back seat, Madeline

slid into the driver's side. "I wish we would hear something from Chloe," Abree said while digging to the bottom of her purse. She came up with a pack of gum and offered Madeline a piece.

"Me too. It's really not like her to be so, you know, silent. Kent used to call her Magpie when she was little because she was always squawking. She must be dealing with something big. I don't know if she ever really dealt with her father's death. I was such a mess, and she stepped in to take care of me. Maybe she never found closure," Madeline said as she turned left at Clara's mailbox.

Abree leaned forward to look out the windshield at the thick pines casting shadows across a narrow strip of green. "I'm really not seeing a road here."

"Just the way Clara likes it," Madeline answered.

Clara sat on the front porch and rose to greet her visitors. As she eyed the bag Madeline handed her, a wide grin lit her tanned face. Madeline introduced Abree as she awkwardly crutched her way across the uneven ground. "I zigged when I should have zagged."

Clara laughed. "Happens to the best of us. I'm having some mint sun tea. Please join me." After the women were seated at the small kitchen table, Clara said, "I was down at Schmidt's this morning. Charlene was telling me about Chloe." Reaching across the table, Clara patted Madeline's arm. "I would have come if I'd known."

"I know you would have. But thankfully everything

turned out okay."

Clara leaned forward. "Have you heard any more from her?"

Shaking her head, Madeline said, "Nothing since the one text."

Clara reached out and laid a blue-veined hand on Madeline's arm. "Sometimes a person just needs time away to think." Refilling Abree's glass, she said, "I have a bountiful garden harvest this year and would like to share. Abree, the ground is very uneven, so I think it would be best if you stayed here. We won't be long."

Left behind, Abree studied the interior of the one-room cabin. A wood cookstove dominated the center of the room. The kitchen table with a bench seat sat beneath a window facing a fenced garden, and a recliner and twin bed shared the opposite wall. A small table within easy reach sat between the two. Abree noticed something small, dark, and round sticking out from under the bed. Curious, she checked to make sure the two women were still in the garden before reaching underneath the bed to feel for the object. She pulled it toward her. Startled, she fell against the bed. The engraved B in a circle on the gun's stock seemed to stare back at her like two large, close-set eyes in a small round face.

* * *

Saturday evening

Troy heard the squawk of blue jays before he reached his camp and wondered what had upset them. He knew he could dismantle his camp in under ten minutes, but darkness would descend before he could reach his Jeep. And even then, he wasn't sure what to do or where to go with what he had found. He remembered the "Wanted— Your Vote" poster for Wayne Sinclair hanging in the Conoco station. If he was running against Sheriff Butler, it stood to reason he wasn't in the Butler cover-up camp. He'd drive the thirty miles to Copperville and call on the wannabe sheriff.

Approaching his camp, Troy glanced up at the tree he'd slung his canvas food bag in. The bag was missing. He hadn't seen any bear signs during the short time he'd been on the mountain, but that didn't mean they weren't around. The sight of his camp, though, stopped him dead in his tracks. The down filling of his sleeping bag and jacket littered the ground like fake snow in a Hollywood film. Shredded bits of his camo tent blended with the forest floor litter. Camp robbers fought for their share of spilled food, and a chipmunk darted away with a cracker. A closer search of the campsite revealed nothing was salvageable. *Unless a bear has learned to use a knife, this is a clear warning from a two-legged critter.*

He dug into his backpack and pulled out the headlamp. He checked to make sure it worked before slipping it onto his head. He hoped with the full moon he could keep the lamp off. He didn't want to advertise where he was, but, remembering Abree's fall, he also didn't want to risk serious injury stumbling around in the dark.

Madeline declined help with the dishes, urging Vince to entertain Abree. "I'll just be stacking them in the dishwasher," Madeline said, smiling up at Vince. "You'd only be in my way. It's such a beautiful evening, I'll make some coffee and we'll sit on the porch."

Vince made sure Abree's leg was elevated before he took a chair next to her.

"Thank you."

"You're welcome."

"I mean thank you for spending time with Madeline. Chloe had told me she was worried about her mother, about her withdrawing more and more since her husband died. I didn't realize just how isolated she had become before I came here. But I watch her around you and … oh, I don't know, it's like she's coming alive again. I wish Chloe would contact us. Or better yet just come home. I just don't understand. We've never kept secrets from each other. Or at least I thought we didn't."

Vince leaned over and took Abree's hand. "Sometimes people just don't know how to share what's going on in their lives. But if you give them time, they'll figure it out."

"Clara said the same thing today." Abree wiggled

circulation back into her toes. "Have you heard from Troy?"

Chuckling, Vince asked, "Worried about your knight in shining armor?"

Abree rolled her eyes at Vince as Madeline joined them with coffee and cookies. Taking the tray, he asked, "How would you ladies like a little adventure? My side-by-side is out front, gassed up and ready to go. I say we pack up these cookies, pour the coffee into thermoses, and take a moonlight drive. It's a full moon tonight," Vince said, wiggling his eyebrows at Madeline. "Bet I can find Troy's camp, and I'm sure he wouldn't turn down a homemade cookie."

Madeline clapped her hands. "I'll make some sandwiches too," she said. "This will be so much fun!"

"I'm glad you brought the blanket," Madeline said tucking it around her and Abree's legs. "It's kind of chilly up here."

Whispering in Madeline's ear, Vince said, "You can get a little closer if you'd like."

A strobe-like effect was created as the side-by-side passed by trees backlit by the bright moonlight. "This is the first time I've ever been in the woods at night," Abree said. "It's like every tree looks like a guy holding a gun. Honestly, it's a little scary."

Kaboom!

Madeline and Abree screamed, and Vince yelled at Abree to get down. He slammed the ATV into park and bailed out, dragging Madeline with him. A second shot brought a branch from above Vince and Madeline crashing down onto them.

The sound of the shot sent Troy into a thicket of gooseberries. The long thorns sliced across the skin of his cheeks and hands. The second shot brought the realization he wasn't the target. Too far away. He fought his way back out of the bushes, getting another slice to his right cheek. He hung tight to the cover lining the trail and headed in the direction of the gunfire. Maybe he could get a description of the shooter.

Vince called out, "Abree, are you okay?"

She answered, "Yes," her voice sounding shaky. "Considering I just got shot at."

Vince raised up, motioning for Madeline to stay down for now. After a few minutes, he helped her up. "Probably some dumb-ass kids shooting at anything that moves. Let's get out of here."

"But what about Troy?" Abree asked. "What if he's hurt or got shot by accident? I think we should make sure he's all right."

"I agree, Vince," Madeline said, wrapping the blanket

to cover herself and Abree again.

Troy fought to control his breathing, nervousness and exertion caused his heart to thump in his chest. He gauged he was close to where the shots had been fired. The distinct rumble of a souped-up muffler echoed behind him, and he dived for cover once again. He watched as the RZR passed him, and he recognized the familiar profile of the sheriff.

He moved swiftly, keeping the taillights of the ATV in sight while staying under cover. He saw the brake lights flash and then a steady red glow. Not slowing his pace, he soon caught up to the machine and stopped, hidden in the thick brush below the trail.

"Evening, Sheriff," Vince said, a hint of strain in his voice.

"Vince, ladies," Jessie responded. "Kind of late for a drive, isn't it?"

"Just showing off our little slice of heaven. Nothing more beautiful than Pewter Creek Mountain under a full moon. But we ran into a little problem."

"What would that be? Out of gas?"

"No, a little more serious than that. Some kids target practicing. Got a little too close for comfort."

"That's what brought me out here. I've been getting reports of gunplay—folks shooting up signs and anything else that moves. Thought I'd try to catch them in the act."

"Well, they sure spoiled our fun. I'm taking the women back to town where it's safe."

Abree sat forward toward Vince, "But what about—"

Vince leaned on the horn, "Oops. Glad to hear you're out doing your job, Sheriff. County getting their money's worth tonight," he chuckled. "Take care, now."

"You do the same," Jessie said, driving around them.

Abree stared accusingly at Vince, "Why didn't you ask her to help us find Troy? He could be really hurt."

Troy stepped out of the bushes and walked to the side-by-side. He leaned into the vehicle, the full moon illuminating his face. "I didn't know you cared."

Abree jumped, then cried, "Troy, your face! You're hurt?"

"I'm going to break up this touching reunion between you two and say it's time to get off this mountain," Vince said, stepping around to stand beside Troy and slapping him on the back. "Troy, help the cripple up on your lap. It'll be a cozy trip down the hill, but I think we'd be wise to leave sooner than later."

Vince rested his hand on Madeline's knee. A dead-center thump into a pothole bumped Abree's injured knee into the dash. She led out a small cry, and Troy readjusted his arms around her. She snuggled against his chest.

Moonlight bathed Madeline's driveway as the four returned to her house. Vince held out his hand to help Madeline out of the side-by-side, then they gathered up the food and walked to the house. Troy picked Abree up and started toward the house.

"I can walk," she said. "I'm not crippled."

"Just thought you wanted to get into the house before next Christmas," Troy said, grinning, as he deposited Abree on the porch.

"What were you doing on the mountain?" Abree asked.

"Tomorrow will be soon enough to talk. Madeline's dead on her feet, and so are you. Good night, Abree," he said as he turned and strode back to the ATV. After a quick peck on Madeline's cheek, Vince joined him.

"We need to talk," Troy said.

"In the famous words of Walt Longmire, 'boy howdy,'" Vince replied.

Troy heard the clink of ice against glass as he walked down the hallway from the bathroom. A bottle of Pendleton and two tumblers sat on the kitchen table. Vince poured two healthy shots in each glass, and Troy gladly took one as he sat down. "I would have liked to retrieve my Jeep tonight, but it seemed like it might have been a risky undertaking."

"Personally, I'm a fan of doing things in daylight." Motioning to Troy's face, he asked, "You tangle with a cougar?"

"Just dived for cover when I heard shots."

"Oh, yeah, them. Apparently, we were the intended targets."

"Who do you think was the shooter?"

"Maybe some kids. Maybe someone else. Whoever shot at us was either a poor shot or a damned good one. Either way, too close for comfort."

"A little coincidental, the sheriff showing up when she did."

Vince picked up his glass, took a sip, and set it on the scarred wooden tabletop. "I get the feeling you don't like our local top dog."

"She certainly doesn't leave me with a warm and fuzzy feeling. And my camp was vandalized. Seemed personal." Troy drained his glass in one gulp and tilted the bottle for another splash. "And there's something else."

It was close to midnight when the two men said goodnight after making plans for the next morning.

CHAPTER 23

Sunday morning

CLARA BRUNNER LEFT HER CABIN as the eastern sky began to lighten. The forest was whisper-quiet, as the night creatures had retreated to their lairs, and the day-dwellers were just beginning to stir. For the first time since Clara had carved out her space on Pewter Creek Mountain, she was afraid. She struggled to maintain her normal gait on familiar paths, stopping every few steps to listen for the now-familiar whine of Zane's RZR.

She'd heard the machine pass by last night on its way up the mountain. In a rash decision, she had pulled the rifle from under the bed and left the cabin. As she tracked the noise, retribution for the death of Rickey played through her thoughts. Her plan was to shoot in the air to scare Zane off the mountain, just to give him a little taste of his own medicine.

She couldn't move in the dark as fast as the ATV and had had to stop several times to listen and get her bearings. The gun was heavier than her deer-hunting .30-30, and the extra weight pulled her off balance. She stumbled and nearly fell several times. She'd heard a machine's growl up ahead to the right and taken her shot, centering on the full moon. Her second shot went wild. The crack of exploding wood was loud, followed by screams. Clara had been startled to see the side-by-side stopped ahead of her. She had heard the noise of the RZR getting close, then stop. Sheriff Butler was driving it, not Zane, as Clara had expected. She watched as the sheriff talked with Vince, Madeline, and Abree.

Clara had been confused by the sheriff's presence. Was Jessie, not Zane, the one who had shot Rickey? Had she made multiple trips past Clara's driveway at all hours of the day and night since Monday night? Had she been the one who had tossed the engraved rifle aside, left in the brush for Clara to find? It seemed out of character but....

No matter who the players were in the shooting game, Clara knew she would have no peace until the gun was out of her hands. And she knew the exact spot to hide the killing machine—a cave created by the rockslide at Big Rumble.

The August sun was warm, and the gun was tiring to carry. She felt queasy and sweaty from lack of sleep, and she'd been unable to eat this morning. The memory of almost killing someone the night before played over and over in her head. She was nearing her destination when voices carried to her on the breeze.

"That's her all right," Vince confirmed, standing upwind of the rocky grave. "Poor Madeline. This is going to be tough on her." He looked over at Troy. "Obviously, this wasn't an accident."

Troy nodded in agreement. "My gut's telling me the sheriff had something to do with it."

"You made some valid points last night."

"It has been a strange chain of events since I rolled into your quiet little town. First the sheriff warns me off going up on the mountain. Then I get hustled off to jail. But I was never charged. Hell, I wasn't even questioned. Then the missing woman texts her mother, but as you pointed out, anyone could have sent that. When I was being processed out, I overheard a call Geraldine made to Ray, the search dog handler. The sheriff had canceled the hound on the first day of searching, not after the text from Chloe. Next, I followed FS 222 to where it intersects with FS 186. It was supposed to be closed by a rockslide, but lo and behold—no slide area. But I did find a gut-shot deer and a beer can—Black Tooth Bomber Mountain. And these. I forgot to show you last night." Troy reached into his left jeans pocket and pulled out the shell casings.

"I know someone partial to that brand of beer. And coincidentally he owns a rifle that shoots that caliber of ammo."

"And speaking of gunplay, who do you think the shooter was last night? The sheriff?"

"Possibly. It was too dark to see if she had a weapon with her, but no one goes up on the mountain without some protection."

"Another thing. My compass came up missing after my search and seizure. It'd sure be a handy piece of evidence to plant at the scene of the crime."

Vince grimaced and shook his head. "All this makes me feel even better about calling in Wayne Sinclair to investigate. Jessie's like a mama grizzly bear when it comes to Zane. If she's covering for him, no one is safe. Let's head up to the road. Wayne should be coming along shortly."

"Mom, I don't see why we are back on the mountain. And why did I have to come with you," Zane whined as they passed Iron Trailhead and started up FS 222. "I'm sick of looking for the gun. Why didn't you bring Eldon instead?"

Jessie hadn't intended to include Zane on the trip this morning, but after her visit to Big Rumble last night she knew she needed help to rebury Chloe. Eldon, again, wasn't answering his phones, and his house had been empty when Jessie swung by.

Using the missing gun as an excuse, she said, "I'm worried about the rifle. I figure if we drive around a little more, it might jog your memory as to where you were." Jessie fingered the outline of the compass in her pocket. The shotgun bumped her leg as Zane drove across a pothole. Jessie touched the burner pistol in her holster. "Mary Beth still at her mother's?"

"Till Monday. The church bazaar was yesterday and of course church today. They have a big dinner and then something again tonight." He looked over at his mother. "Were you ever sorry you got married?"

Jessie bought time before answering by cracking open her water bottle. "Oh, I wouldn't say sorry as much as disappointed. My life certainly hasn't gone as I had planned." She took a drink. "You never deposited money into my account," she said. "Are we in trouble, financially, at the store?"

"Sort of."

"How much sort of?"

"Bunches."

The sound of a motor carried up the canyon walls. "I thought you said Wayne wouldn't be able to get here for another hour," Troy said.

"Maybe he put the pedal to the metal. But that sounds

like an ATV. Wayne would be driving a pickup."

Troy, head down, concentrated on his footing as he took a direct route up the loose shale to the road. Vince began to follow. After Troy lost his footing and slipped backwards, Vince hollered, "Sure you don't want to take the easier trail?"

Troy answered, "Faster this way."

An overhang of small pines hid the road surface from above for the last few feet of the ascent. Troy grasped a spindly pine for leverage, his head coming even with the roadbed.

And even with the barrel of a shotgun, the sound of a round being chambered.

CHAPTER 24

"CLIMB UP HERE, THE BOTH OF YOU," Sheriff Butler said, keeping the gun level with Troy's chest.

"Morning, Sheriff," Vince said.

Addressing Troy, Jessie said, "You just can't help yourself, always poking around where you don't belong."

Zane came toward the three, zipping up as he walked. "Hey, Vince, what's shaking?" he asked, his mother's back blocking the gun she held on Troy.

Vince said, "Just doing some fishing."

"Without poles?" the sheriff asked.

Vince shrugged. Unsnapping her holster, she handed the burner pistol to Zane. "Cover Vince. We're going to take a little walk."

"Mom, what are you doing?" Zane asked, holding his hands up and backing away from his mother.

"Just do as I say," Jessie handed Zane the pistol. "You and I were out here having a little bonding time and heard two shots fired. By the time we got to these two, they were both dead. An open-and-shut case of murder/suicide. I did a little research on our ex-soldier boy, Troy Edwards. After his tour of duty ended, he moved to live near his buddy, Trace Richards, to help with his rehab. Guess you can say it didn't work out so well. Trace ended up dead of a gunshot to the head. Local authorities investigated, and they questioned whether it was really a suicide, since Troy was on the scene. According to the police report it was a touching scene—Troy holding Trace in his arms. Shrink's report included in the file said both veterans had been diagnosed with PTSD. Never can tell what will set a sufferer off. I guess it's as good an excuse as any."

Troy lunged at the sheriff. "Don't you dare make light of his death."

Jessie fired a round, narrowly missing Troy's boot-clad foot. "Don't you dare make me shoot you before it's time. Now head up the road, both of you."

A whirlwind from below swirled across them, bringing with it the smell of death. "Whew! Something dead down there," Zane said, waving the air in front of his nose.

Troy stopped and turned to catch Vince's raised eyebrows.

"Troy, I'm warning you. Get moving up the road. There's a trail to the left. But I guess you two know all about it. But do you know about the cave?"

Clara watched as the four made their way down the trail. Sunlight bounced off the weapon Zane held pointed at Vince. Jessie prodded the other man along with a shotgun.

Vince has always been kind to me, Clara thought.

And now it looks like he's in trouble. She lifted the heavy gun and rested it in the crook of a tree, tracking the four as they made their way down the gully, closer and closer to her hiding place.

Sweat beaded up on Troy's upper lip. He called over his shoulder, "Zane, Chloe's death was an accident, wasn't it?"

"Shut up," Jessie said.

But Troy didn't listen. He kept talking. "Mama helped like she always does. But it was an accident, not murder. If you pull the trigger now, though, it'll be murder. And when you're caught, you'll be someone's bitch in jail. Probably passed around, as pretty as you are."

Jessie charged forward, jabbing the barrel of the gun into Troy's back with enough force to slam him to the ground. "I told you to shut up."

Vince took up where Troy left off. "Sheriff, too bad it's not hunting season. You could pass everything off as an accidental shooting. You know how to set that up, don't you? Poor old Rodney didn't see it coming."

Zane turned to face his mother, "What's he talking about?"

Jessie swung the rifle off Troy and pointed it at Vince's face. "Shut your pie hole, or I'll shut it for you. The next one of you that sneezes won't be here long enough to hear 'God bless you,'" Jessie said, refocusing the gun on Troy. "Now get moving."

The climb to the cave became laborious. Troy picked a path and was followed closely by Jessie. Vince grunted as he picked his way through the river of rocks up the steep grade.

Zane's slick-bottomed sneakers afforded him little traction on the loose shale, and he fell, sliding backwards. "I don't think I can make it." His words came in stilted huffs.

"We're almost there. Just a little farther." Jessie spoke as if she was urging a baby to take another step.

The four crested a small summit, which leveled out to a rock apron in front of the cave entrance. The echo of a vehicle door slamming carried across from the road. They watched as two men came to stand beside the left front fender. The red letters *Elect Sinclair for Sheriff* stood out bold on the white vehicle. The four watched as a whirlwind twisted through the brush below, climbing to

145

knock the cowboy hat off one of the men. The other pointed toward the rockslide.

Vince bent over, hands on his knees, and gulped air. Zane rubbed his rib cage like a child with a stitch in his side. Jessie stood breathing hard, her gun once again pointed at Troy's chest.

Zane took a step toward his mother. "What did Vince mean about Dad's hunting accident?"

"Just a ploy to distract you, son. It's the oldest trick in the book—get your captors arguing amongst themselves. But you and me, we are in this together. Everything I've ever done has been for you. Just remember that."

Vince, having caught his breath, spoke up. "That's right, Zane. Your dad was always the third wheel, ever since her little baby boy was born."

Jessie fired back. "Rodney Butler was a weak excuse for a man."

"Did that really mean he had to die, Jessie?" Vince asked.

They all heard sirens in the distance.

"I warned you, Vince, to keep your pie hole shut."

Vince, unfazed, continued, "Zane's not a little boy anymore, Jessie. You need to tell him. You and he are in it together, right? He needs to know all the cards before the house you've built comes tumbling down."

"Mom?"

"Your father ruined us with his gambling. And he wasn't ever going to stop. No matter how many times he promised, it was always the same story—'I thought the slot machine was about to pay out … the pony was a sure thing … my point spread was right on until the interception.' He gambled one last time that I wouldn't follow through with my threat—and lost."

"The day he died," Zane said, slowly, "you said you were too sick to go hunting. He went by himself. But I called the house because I'd forgotten my geometry book, and you didn't answer. I just thought you were in the bathroom or something."

The whine of the sirens echoed louder in the canyon. "Sounds like the cavalry is coming," Troy announced.

"But sadly, too late. Change of plans. Sorry, Vince. You've just become collateral damage in my shootout with the stranger who killed our local girl, Chloe Granger."

Jessie swung the shotgun at Vince's chest and racked in a shell.

A shot cracked in the air. Clara stepped around from behind a boulder, Heym raised, Zane her target. "Jessie Marie Butler, if Vince dies, your little boy does too."

Jessie whirled around, focusing the shotgun on Clara. Troy launched at Jessie, knocking her forward. The gun discharged as she fell, a smattering of pellets tearing into Zane's shoulder.

CHAPTER 25

THE TOWN WAS ABUZZ with what the officials were calling the "Pewter Creek Mountain Incident." Vince had not left Madeline's side since he and Troy had been allowed to leave the incident command center, which had been set up in the meeting room of the library. The sheriff's office had been sealed, pending an investigation of Sheriff Butler's files—all sixteen years.

As Vince had predicted, the news of Chloe's death had devastated Madeline. A roller coaster of emotions whirled through the Granger home. Troy and Abree hovered on the periphery, feeling useless.

Midafternoon, Clara had walked unannounced into the kitchen where the four of them sat pushing food around on their plates. Vince pushed back his chair and walked over to embrace the woman. She moved to stand beside Madeline and addressed the room. "I would like some time with Madeline alone, please. I understand loss." Madeline took Clara's outstretched hand and followed her, zombie-like, down the hall and into her bedroom. The click of the door shutting was loud in the silent house.

"Well, I could use some personal hygiene time," Vince said. "Call if you need anything. On second thought, Troy, the last time you called, I nearly died," Vince said, chuckling.

"Well, you didn't keep your pie hole shut, as I recall. Brought it on yourself."

Abree pushed her chair back. She struggled to stand, and pain pinched her face when she hit her injured knee on the table leg. "How can you two joke about nearly dying?" she asked angrily.

"I'll let you answer that one, Troy," Vince said, exiting the room.

Uncomfortable silence filled the space. Minutes passed before Abree said, "I'm waiting for an answer."

Troy shrugged. "I guess maybe you had to be there. I don't really have a good answer. I'm sure some head-shrinker could give you a fancy name for it—some syndrome."

"Like PTSD?"

Troy studied the brown liquid in the cup in front of

him. Without looking up, he said, "Vince has a big mouth."

Abree touched Troy's hand, "It doesn't matter to me. It was in the past."

"But the past doesn't always stay buried."

Abree's cell phone sang out, cutting off what she was about to say. "Speaking of the past." She answered, "Hello, Dan," as she stepped out the back door.

Troy touched the area on his hand where, only moments before, Abree's warmth had penetrated. Her fragrance remained. He glanced out the kitchen window and watched as she paced, cell phone tight to her ear. He cleaned the kitchen up, while she remained outside, talking to her husband.

Troy moved into the living room and collapsed onto the sofa. He pulled the compass from his pocket, relieved the authorities had seen no reason to keep it for evidence against Jessie. He fingered Trace's initials. *Well, buddy, your compass sure got me into a whole lot of hot water. But maybe it helped me find someone to move forward with in my life.*

Troy drifted off as the light from the muted television danced across the room. He came awake with a start as the couch cushion indented next to him. Abree offered him a steaming cup of coffee.

"Troy, I'm not a quitter."

"Good to know."

"I take marriage vows seriously."

"Also good to know."

"I'm going home to my husband tomorrow."

"Not so good to know."

Abree stood. "I have to pack."

She had reached the doorway when Troy called out, "Abree."

"Yes?"

"I'll wait for your call."

"Good to know."

EPILOGUE

October

Highland City, Colorado

ABREE ANSWERED HER CELL on the second ring. "Hello, Madeline."

"We'll see you tonight?"

"Yes. I'll be there by late afternoon."

"Clara's expecting you to pick her up by six so you can get to the Penwells' place before six-thirty. Geraldine insisted on cooking the rehearsal dinner with one stipulation—Ernest likes to eat his dinner at six-thirty sharp. Be aware that he will likely corner you and rant about how he hopes that the low-down, dirty skunk of a sheriff and her weasel of a son hang from the tallest tree on Pewter Creek Mountain. And just so you know, Clara might grumble a bit too. She's not completely on board with moving to Vince's house for the winter. But he was able to persuade her he didn't want his water freezing, and since she doesn't have running water at her cabin it's not an issue for her. Don't forget your dress."

"Already in the car. And the matching shoes. I have to go. The movers are here."

"Call me when you leave."

"Will do. And Madeline?" Abree's voice grew thick. "Chloe would be so happy for you. Vince is a great guy."

"She would, wouldn't she," Madeline answered.

A half-hour later, Abree walked into the now-empty house she had shared with Dan. Most of the home's furnishings had been sold, save for a few pieces that had been in her family for generations. The moving men had stowed the furniture in her storage unit and offered to help Abree with the few boxes in her car. She thanked them, but declined, needing time alone. She'd rolled the unit door down with a bang before the empty feelings of a failed marriage overtook her with tears once again.

She'd returned to the house, just planning to pick up the last of her things—to close this chapter of her life. But instead she pulled the manila envelope from her tote bag and spread clippings from *The Cobalt County News* across the counter. Madeline had faithfully sent Abree updates since Jessie and Zane had been hauled off the mountain in handcuffs. Because there seemed to be some confusion about what exactly the two were being charged with, they were currently out on their own recognizance. Pending the investigation, Sheriff Butler and Deputy Eldon Johnson had been relieved of their duties. Wayne Sinclair had been appointed sheriff in the interim, and he was now running unopposed in the November election. Zane's injuries had been superficial, and his wife, Mary Beth, remained faithfully at his side.

Abree blinked tears away seeing the smiling face of Chloe Granger underneath the heading "Obituaries." She set the tribute to her friend aside to look at the picture of Curtis Winslow, owner, and Vince, new store manager, standing in front of Pewter Creek Hardware. Enthusiasm bubbled from Madeline during their weekly phone calls as she updated Abree on all the changes she was helping Vince make to the rebranded Butler's Sporting Goods Store.

Madeline had sent two clippings last week. One was a thank you from the Moody Search and Rescue crew, Jake, Sterling, and Wade, to the residents of Pewter Creek for the benefit supper and silent auction held to help defray medical costs resulting from the accident they had suffered during the search for Chloe. Sterling was still side-lined from the team until his shoulder completely healed, but Jake and Wade were cleared for duty.

The second clipping, dated last week, showed a grainy photo of Eldon Johnson staring back at her from a grayscale box with the headline "Former Deputy Found Dead." The suspended deputy had been rumored to be turning state's evidence against his former boss and her son concerning the death of Chloe Granger, but he had been found by some mountain bikers off FS 222, a bottle of Jim Beam and a burner pistol beside his dead body.

Madeline had told Abree that she wished the Butlers would throw themselves on the mercy of the court and get this entire thing over with. But Vince said Jessie was no quitter, and she must be figuring that she and Zane would get off on a technicality now that Eldon was conveniently out of the picture.

Quitter.

Abree had told Troy she wasn't a quitter.

She'd returned to her marriage, to Dan, and been caught up in his whirlwind of ideas. Instead of a vacation, he kicked off his gubernatorial campaign. He hired a personal trainer, reassuring her that her hard work would pay off with a slimmer, sexier new Abree. He'd pulled some strings to get her a job with a nonprofit organization. "Looks good on my resume," he had said. And they were on the fast track for the adoption of twins—a girl and a boy.

But then she had accepted a lunch invitation from Dan's former assistant—pushy, petite Sarah. Before the entree was even served, Sarah had dropped the bombshell about the affair she and Dan had been having.

Dan had seemed truly shocked when Abree filed for divorce.

The sound of the house keys being laid on the granite kitchen counter echoed in the empty house. Abree gathered her suitcase, tote, and purse and shut the door on her past, checking to make sure the latch caught.

The Welcome to Pewter Creek sign came into view, looking festive with fall decorations. Abree fumbled in her purse for her cell phone and searched her contact list.

On the second ring, a voice answered, "Hello."

"Troy, I'm calling."

"Good to know."

The End

ABOUT THE AUTHOR

Sundance Mountain, Black Buttes, O'Haver Hill, Inyan Kara Mountain

Kathy "K.D." Gearhart grew up on a ranch south of
Sundance, Wyoming with the above geological formations as
her playground. Now retired and living just across the
Wyoming border in Spearfish, South Dakota, she draws
inspiration for her suspense novels from driving the back roads
of the Wyoming and South Dakota Black Hills.

For more work by K.D. Gearhart, please check
her Amazon Page:
https://www.amazon.com/K.-D.-Gearhart/e/B07RS4JLZ5/

Or send her an email at: gearhartkd@gmail.com

Made in the USA
Lexington, KY
30 September 2019